BEFORE YOUR MEMORY FADES

Also by Toshikazu Kawaguchi

Before the coffee gets cold
Tales from the cafe
Before we say goodbye

Toshikazu Kawaguchi

BEFORE YOUR MEMORY FADES

Translated from the Japanese by Geoffrey Trousselot

PICADOR

First published 2022 by Picador

This edition first published by Picador 2023
an imprint of Pan Macmillan
The Smithson, 6 Briset Street, London ECIM 5NR
EU representative: Macmillan Publishers Ireland Ltd, 1st Floor,
The Liffey Trust Centre, 117–126 Sheriff Street Upper,
Dublin 1, DOI YC43
Associated companies throughout the world
www.panmacmillan.com

ISBN 978-1-0350-3240-2

Copyright © Toshikazu Kawaguchi 2018

Translation copyright © Sunmark Publishing, Inc. 2022

The right of Toshikazu Kawaguchi to be identified as the
author of this work has been asserted by him in accordance
with the Copyright, Designs and Patents Act 1988.

Originally published in Japan as OMOIDE GA KIENAI UCHI NI
by Sunmark Publishing Inc., Tokyo, Japan in 2018
Japanese/English translation rights arranged with Sunmark
Publishing, Inc., through Gudovitz & Company Literary
Agency, New York, USA

1 3 5 7 9 8 6 4 2

A CIP catalogue record for this book is available from the British Library.

Typeset in Giovanni by Jouve (UK), Milton Keynes
Printed and bound by CPI Group (UK) Ltd, Croydon, CRO 4YY

Visit **www.picador.com** to read more about all our books
and to buy them. You will also find features, author interviews and
news of any author events, and you can sign up for e-newsletters
so that you're always first to hear about our new releases.

If you could go back, who would you want to meet?

Relationship map of characters

Old gentleman in black

A ghost who sits at the table closest to the entrance, in the seat that allows you to time travel. He leaves the seat once a day to go to the toilet.

Kohta Hayashida

A comedian who with Gen Todoroki makes up the successful comedy duo PORON DORON.

Gen Todoroki

A comedian who with Kohta Hayashida makes up the successful comedy duo PORON DORON. His wife, Setsuko Yoshioka, died five years ago.

Keiichi Seto

Father of Yayoi Seto.

Yayoi Seto

A young woman whose parents died in a car crash when she was six.

Setsuko Yoshioka

The wife of Gen Todoroki. She died five years ago.

Miyuki Seto

Mother of Yayoi Seto. She died in a car crash when Yayoi was six.

came from the past

returns to the past

returns to the past

Yukari Tokita

The former owner of Donna Donna. She is away in America helping a boy find his father.

Sachi Tokita

Daughter of Kazu Tokita, aged seven. She serves the coffee during the ceremony that allows people to time travel.

came from the past

returns to the past

Reiji Ono

A university student and aspiring comedian who works at Donna Donna. Childhood friend of Nanako Matsubara.

Nagare Tokita

Father of Miki Tokita, son of Yukari Tokita. Running his mother's Donna Donna cafe, owns Funiculi Funicula in Tokyo. His wife, Kei, died fifteen years ago giving birth to Miki.

Kazu Tokita

Cousin of Nagare Tokita. Mother of Sachi. She is working at Donna Donna while Yukari Tokita is away.

Reiko Nunokawa

A regular customer at Donna Donna. Her younger sister Yukika died a few months ago.

Dr Saki Muraoka

A hospital psychiatrist and regular customer at Donna Donna.

Nanako Matsubara

A university student and regular customer at Donna Donna. Childhood friend of Reiji Ono.

Yukika Nunokawa

Younger sister of Reiko Nunokawa. She worked part-time in Donna Donna and died a few months ago.

CONTENTS

I

The Daughter

'Why are you in Hokkaido?'

Kei Tokita's voice sounded tinny coming from the handset.

'Hey, relax, it's OK.'

Nagare Tokita was hearing his wife's voice for the first time in fourteen years. He was in Hokkaido – Hakodate, to be exact.

The city of Hakodate is full of Western-style houses, dating from the early twentieth century. Those houses, dotted throughout the city, have a unique architectural style, characterized by Japanese ground floors and Western upper floors. The Motomachi area (whose name means 'original town'), located at the very base of Mount Hakodate, is a popular tourist destination. Its old-town charm is enhanced by such popular historic sites as the former public hall, a rectangular concrete electricity pole – the first ever erected in Japan – and the red-brick warehouses in its historical Bay Area.

Kei, on the other end of the phone line, was far away in Tokyo, at a certain cafe that offered its customers the chance to travel through time. It was called Funiculi Funicula. She had travelled fifteen years into the future from the past in order to meet her daughter. In that Tokyo cafe, she only had a brief time before she had to drink her cooling coffee. As he was far away in Hokkaido, in northern Japan, Nagare had no idea how far her coffee had cooled already. He was therefore careful to stick to the matter at hand.

'There's no time to explain why I'm in Hokkaido. Please, just listen.'

Of course, Kei was well aware that there was no time.

'What's that? There's no time? I'm the one with no time!' She sounded upset.

But Nagare paid no attention. 'A girl is there, right? Who looks like she might be in middle school.'

'What? A schoolgirl? Yes, she's here. The same one who visited the cafe about two weeks ago; she came from the future to get a photo with me.'

It had been two weeks ago for Kei, but she was referring to something that for Nagare happened a whole fifteen years ago.

'She's got big round eyes . . . and she's wearing a turtle-neck?'

'Yes, yes. What about her?'

'OK, just calm down and listen. You've accidentally travelled fifteen years into the future.'

'Like I told you, I can hardly hear what you're saying.'

A howling gust of wind had struck Nagare just as he was about to tell her something crucial. It was blowing a gale down his phone, making it next to impossible to communicate. Pressed by the lack of time, Nagare hurried.

'Anyway, that girl you're looking at,' he said, louder.

'Eh? What? That girl?'

'She's our daughter!'

'What?'

The phone in Nagare's hands fell completely silent. Then instead of Kei's voice, he heard the middle pendulum clock in Funiculi Funicula begin chiming a familiar *dong, dong*. Letting out a small sigh, he began explaining calmly.

'You agreed to travel ten years into the future, so you think that your child will be about ten, but there was some kind of mistake and you travelled fifteen years. It seems ten years fifteen hours and fifteen years ten hours got mixed up. Just look at the time of the middle pendulum clock. It says ten o'clock, right?'

'Uh-huh.'

'We heard about it when you got back. But right now, we are in Hokkaido for unavoidable reasons that I won't go into because there's no time.'

Nagare had rattled through this explanation. But now he paused.

'Anyway, you don't have much time left, so just have a good look at our all-grown-up, fit-and-well daughter and return to your present,' he said gently and hung up.

From where he was standing, Nagare could see all the way down the straight, sloping street to the sprawling blueness of the ocean, and the sky beyond which seemed to crown Hakodate Port. He swung back on his heel and walked into the cafe.

DA-DING-DONG

Hakodate boasts many sloping streets. Nineteen of them have been given names, including Twenty Astride Rise, which stretches up from Japan's oldest electricity pole, and Eight Banner Rise, which starts near the red-brick warehouses of Hakodate's touristy Bay Area. Others include Fish View Rise and Ship View Rise, which climb from the Hakodate waterfront. Further over the hillside are Cockle Rise and Green Willow Rise, which climb towards Yachigashiracho, meaning head of the valley. But there is one sloping street that the tourist maps don't show. Locals refer to it as No Name Rise. The cafe where Nagare was working was halfway up No Name Rise.

Its name was Cafe Donna Donna, and a peculiar urban legend was attached to a particular seat in that cafe.

Apparently, if you sat on that seat, it would take you back in time to whenever you wanted.

But the rules were extremely annoying and a terrible nuisance:

1. The only people you can meet in the past are those who have visited the cafe.
2. There is nothing you can do while in the past that will change the present.
3. In order to return to the past, you have to sit in that seat and that seat alone. If the seat is occupied, you must wait until it is vacated.
4. While back in the past, you must stay in the seat and never move from it.

5. Your journey begins when the coffee is poured and must end before the coffee gets cold.

The annoying rules don't end there either. Be that as it may, today once again, a customer who has heard this rumour will visit the cafe.

When Nagare returned from his phone call, Nanako Matsubara, sitting at one of the counter stools, came straight out and asked, 'Nagare, why didn't you stay in Tokyo? Do you still think it was a good idea to come here?'

Nanako was a student at Hakodate University. Wearing her light beige top tucked into her baggy trousers, she looked kind of trendy. Her make-up was lightly applied, her hair, loosely permed and tied back with a scrunchie.

Nanako had heard that Nagare's deceased wife would be visiting from the past to meet her daughter at the Tokyo cafe. Considering it was a one-time-only chance to meet the wife he had not seen for fourteen years, Nanako thought it was strange Nagare decided to greet her over the phone rather than see her in person.

'Yeah, maybe,' Nagare replied vaguely as he walked past her and went behind the counter. On the stool next to Nanako sat a sleepy-looking Dr Saki Muraoka with a book in her hand. Saki worked in the psychiatric department at one of Hakodate's hospitals. Both she and Nanako were cafe regulars.

'Didn't you want to see her again?'

Nanako's inquisitive eyes stayed focused on Nagare, a giant of a man nearly two metres tall.

'Sure, but I had to respect the facts.'

'Which were?'

'She came to see her daughter, not me.'

'But still.'

'It's fine. I admit it has been a while, but my memories are still very much alive . . .'

Nagare meant he would do anything he could to make the time between mother and daughter more precious.

'You are so kind, Nagare,' Nanako said admiringly.

'Jesus!' he retorted, as his ears flushed red.

'No need to get embarrassed.'

'I'm nothing of the sort,' he replied, promptly disappearing into the kitchen to escape her.

Taking his place, Kazu Tokita, the waitress, appeared from the kitchen. Over her white shirt and beige frilly skirt she wore an aqua-blue apron. She was thirty-seven but her free-spirited and happy-go-lucky demeanour gave her the air of a younger person.

'What number question are you up to?'

Now that Kazu was behind the counter again, the subject of the conversation changed.

'Um, question twenty-four.' It was Saki, sitting next to Nanako, who replied. Showing a complete lack of interest in Nanako's conversation with Nagare, Saki had instead been reading her book attentively.

'Oh, yes . . .' Nanako chimed in, as if suddenly remembering. She cast a furtive eye at the book in Saki's hands. Saki flicked back several pages and read aloud.

What If The World Were Ending Tomorrow? One Hundred Questions

Question Twenty-Four

There is a man or woman with whom you are very much in love.

If the world were to end tomorrow, which would you do?

1. You propose to them.

2. You don't propose because there is no point.

'So, which is it?' Saki had pulled her gaze from the book and was looking at Nanako.

'Um, I'm not sure which I would do.'

'Come on, which?'

'Well, which would you do, Saki?'

'Me? I think I would propose.'

'Why?'

'I don't like the idea of dying with regrets.'

'Oh, I guess that's a fair point.'

'Eh? Nanako, are you saying you wouldn't propose?'

Pressed to answer, Nanako tilted her head. 'Oh, I don't know,' she said softly. 'Well, maybe if I knew for certain that he loved me, I would. But if I wasn't sure how he felt, I probably wouldn't.'

'Really? Why not?'

Saki seemed unable to accept what Nanako was saying.

'Well, if I knew he loved me, I wouldn't be presenting him with a dilemma, would I?'

'No, I guess not.'

'But if he had never thought about me in that way before, then proposing would force him to think about me differently, and I would hate to add to his worries.'

'Oh, and that does actually happen, with men, particularly. Like on Valentine's Day when some guy gets chocolate from a woman he has never thought about before. Suddenly he becomes all conscious of her.'

'I'd feel pretty rotten if I caused someone extra worries just at the time the world is about to end. I also wouldn't like it if I didn't get a reply. So, although proposing to someone might be meaningful, I don't think I would do it.'

'I think you're taking it too seriously, Nanako.'

'Oh, really?'

'Definitely! It's not as though the world is ending tomorrow, anyway.'

'Yeah, I guess so.'

This chatter had been shuttling back and forth since before Nagare had gone outside to take the phone call.

'What about you, Kazu, which would you do?' Nanako leaned forward on the counter. Saki also looked towards Kazu with much interest.

'Well, I'd . . .'

DA-DING-DONG

'Hello! Welcome,' Kazu called out automatically in the direction of the entrance upon hearing the bell. In an instant, she put on her waitress face. On seeing that, Nanako and Saki were no longer pressing her to answer the question. But rather than a customer entering the cafe, in walked a girl wearing a light pink dress.

'I'm back!' she called out energetically.

Her name was Sachi Tokita, Kazu's seven-year-old

daughter. She was lugging a heavy looking bag on her shoulder and gripping a postcard in her hand. The postcard was from Koku Shintani, her father and Kazu's husband, who was a world-renowned photographer. He had married into and hence taken the surname of the Tokita family but worked under his own name. His job involved constantly zipping around the world photographing landscapes, and he only spent a few days each year in Japan. Shintani therefore made postcards of the photos he took and frequently sent them to Sachi.

'Welcome back!' greeted Nanako. Kazu was looking behind Sachi at the young man following her in.

'Good morning,' said one Reiji Ono, a part-time employee at the cafe.

Wearing casual attire of denim jeans and white T-shirt, Reiji was a little out of breath. Beads of sweat had formed on his forehead, a clear sign he had climbed the hill in a hurry.

'We just happened to arrive at the same time,' Reiji said to explain why he had entered with Sachi, not that anyone had asked.

Reiji disappeared into the kitchen from where he could be heard greeting Nagare. They were about to begin preparing for the busy lunchtime period, which would start in two hours.

Sachi took a seat at the table next to the large window that commanded a stunning view across Hakodate Port. She appeared to be treating it as her own private study booth.

There were other customers in the cafe besides Nanako and Saki. An old gentleman in a formal black suit was seated at the table closest to the entrance, and a woman roughly the same age as Nanako was at a four-seater table. She had been there since opening time, doing nothing but gazing dreamily out of the window. The cafe opened rather early at seven a.m., to catch the tourists visiting the morning market.

Sachi heaved her bag onto the table. Based on the unexpectedly loud thump, something heavy was obviously inside.

'What's in there? Have you been to the library again?'

'Uh-huh.'

Nanako sat down at the seat opposite her as she talked to Sachi.

'You certainly like books.'

'Uh-huh.'

Nanako knew that on every day Sachi didn't have school, her routine was to visit the library first thing in the morning to borrow books. Today, her elementary school had a special holiday to commemorate its foundation. Sachi gleefully began arranging her newly borrowed books on the table.

'So, what kind of books do you read?'

'Hey, I want to know too! Which books do you like, Sachi?'

Dr Saki Muraoka got off her stool and came over.

'What did you get? What did you get?'

Nanako reached out and picked up one of the books.

'*Imaginary Number and Integer Challenge*.'

Saki did likewise.

'*Apocalypse in a Finite Universe*.'

'*Modern Quantum Mechanics and the Non-Miss Diet*.'

Nanako and Saki took turns reading the titles aloud.

'*Problems of Classical Art Learned from Picasso*.'

'*The Spiritual World of African Textiles*.'

As they picked up each book, the expression vanished from their faces. They were more than a little stunned by the titles. There were still some books whose titles they had not read left on the table, but neither felt like going for them.

'Well, er, they're certainly all very difficult-looking books!' remarked Nanako, wincing.

'Difficult? Are they really?' Sachi tilted her head with uncertainty.

'Sachi darling, if you can understand these books, I think we are going to have to start calling you Dr Sachi!' Saki sighed, staring at *The Spiritual World of African Textiles*. The book was similar to the medical literature that someone like Saki, working in psychiatry, would read.

'She's not interested in understanding them. She just likes looking at all the interesting writing,' said Kazu from behind the counter, as if to console the two adults.

'Even so . . . Right?'

'Yeah . . . Wow.'

The two women wanted to say those weren't books that a seven-year-old girl chooses.

Nanako returned to the counter, picked up the book Saki had been reading and started flicking through the pages.

'A book like this is just right for me.'

She meant that rather than having small text tightly crammed together, this book's text only had a few lines per page.

'What's that you're reading?'

The book seemed to have piqued Sachi's interest as well.

'Do you want to read a little?'

Nanako passed the book to Sachi.

'*What If The World Were Ending Tomorrow? One Hundred Questions*.'

Sachi read the title aloud with her eyes ablaze in excitement.

'That sounds so interesting!'

'Do you want to try it?'

Nanako had brought the book to the cafe, and she was happy that Sachi was showing an interest in it.

'Sure!' Sachi replied with a smile.

'Well, where better to start reading than the first question. Let's say we do that.'

'That's a good idea,' said Nanako. Turning back to the first page, she read out the question.

'"Question One.

'"Right now, in front of you is a room that only one person can enter. If you enter it, you will be saved from the end of the world.

'"If the world were to end tomorrow, which action do you take?

'"1. You enter the room.

'"2. You don't enter the room."

'So, which do you choose?' Nanako's resonant voice carried well.

'Hmmm.'

Sachi knitted her brows. Both Nanako and Saki smiled while they watched Sachi as she seemed to ponder the question seriously. Their smiles were probably born from relief that she was just a seven-year-old girl after all.

'Was that question too hard for you, Sachi?' Nanako asked, studying Sachi's face.

'I wouldn't enter the room,' Sachi declared confidently.

'Oh?' Nanako sounded taken aback by Sachi's unwavering certainty. Nanako had chosen to enter the room, as had Saki beside her. Kazu, still behind the counter, listened to the conversation with a cool expression.

'Why not enter?' Nanako asked. Her voice sounded amazed that a seven-year-old girl would choose to not enter the room.

Seemingly oblivious to how puzzled Nanako and Saki appeared, Sachi sat up straight and stated a reason that for them was unthinkable.

'Well, surviving alone is much the same as dying alone, don't you think?'

'. . .'

The two women were lost for words. With her mouth agape, Nanako looked stunned.

'Sachi, your answer is better than mine!' said Saki, bowing. She had to admit her deference to that answer, which she never would have considered. Nanako and Saki looked at each other with the same thought: *Perhaps that girl actually understands those difficult books she reads!*

'Ah, back doing that again, I see,' remarked Reiji, who had emerged from the kitchen. He was now wearing an apron. 'That book is really popular right now.'

'Well it must be popular if even Reiji has heard of it!' exclaimed Saki.

'What do you mean by "even"?'

'You don't strike me as a big book-reader, that's all.'

'Humph! I'll have you know, I lent it to that woman in the first place.'

Normally it would be impolite to say 'that woman', especially when Nanako was right there beside them. But Reiji had grown up with Nanako and they were both studying at the same university, so he was sometimes a little cheeky when it came to her.

'Oh, really?'

'Yeah, Reiji said it was interesting and lent it to me. The book is really popular around campus.'

'It sounds very popular.'

Dr Saki Muraoka held out her hand as if to say *give me another look*, and Nanako passed it to her.

'Everyone is getting into it.'

'Yes, hmm, I sort of understand why.'

Hearing that it was all the rage made sense to Saki. She too had been engrossed in it until Nagare had gone outside to make his phone call. And just now, it had drawn in seven-year-old Sachi. She thought it would probably become a hit across the country as she took another look through the pages.

'Interesting,' she said admiringly.

'Thank you, that was delicious,' said the young woman who had been there since opening as she stood up from her table. Reiji took little running steps over to the register.

'Iced tea and cake set, right? Seven hundred and eighty yen, please,' he announced after examining the bill.

Without replying, the woman took her purse from her shoulder bag. As she did, unbeknownst to her or anyone else, a single photo fell to the floor.

'OK, here . . .' She handed him a one-thousand-yen note.

'Accepting one thousand yen . . .' The *bip-bip* of the cash register rang out as Reiji tapped its keys. The drawer popped out with a quiet *kerchunk*, and he deftly pulled out the change in a manner that showed he had done it many times before. 'Returning two hundred and twenty change.'

After silently accepting the change from Reiji's outreached hand, she walked towards the door while muttering, as if to herself, 'What that girl said is right. I'd be better off dead than to live life alone.'

DA-DING-DONG

'Thank you . . . for . . . coming . . .'

Reiji did not deliver his send-off as clearly and brightly as he normally did.

'What's up?' asked Saki to Reiji as he was returning from the cash register with his head cocked to the side.

'Er, just now . . . I'd be better off dead!'

'What?' shrieked Nanako in surprise.

'Er, no, no! It was that woman; she said she'd be better off dead than to live life alone,' Reiji added hastily.

'Don't scare me like that!' Nanako said, smacking Reiji on the back as he walked past.

'But still . . .' said a puzzled-looking Saki, appealing to Kazu. The comment was, after all, not something to ignore.

Kazu's eyes were fixed on the entrance. 'Yes . . . quite strange,' she responded.

For a moment, time itself seemed to stop.

'What's the next one?' Sachi asked, bringing everyone back to earth. Her eyes were pleading for them all to continue with *One Hundred Questions*. But Saki looked at the pendulum clock and stood up saying, 'Oh, would you look at the time . . .'

It was ten thirty.

The cafe had three large pendulum clocks, stretching from the floor to the ceiling. One was near the entrance, one in the middle of the cafe, and one next to the large window overlooking Hakodate Port. The clock that Saki used to check the time was the middle one. The clock near the entrance ran fast, and the one next to the window ran slow.

'Time for work?'

'Yes,' confirmed Saki as she pulled out coins from her purse, showing no signs of being in a hurry. She lived just a stone's throw away from the cafe. It had become a daily routine to pop in to drink a coffee before work.

'What about the next question, Dr Saki?'

'Let's do it later, OK?' Saki said with a smile and placed three hundred and eighty yen on the counter.

Reacting to Sachi's somewhat glum face, Kazu said, 'Why don't you start reading those books you borrowed?'

'OK.'

Sachi's expression brightened instantly. Her style of book-reading was to open many at once and read them side by side. She probably looked glum because it was the first time that she had ever shared reading with everyone like that. It had been fun. She snapped out of her glumness as soon as Kazu suggested she read her new books. After all, it was a new chance to enjoy her favourite pastime.

She picked up one of the books spread out at the table seat, plonked herself down on a chair and instantly began reading in silence.

'She does love books,' remarked Nanako a little enviously. She had always struggled to read difficult works.

'Later then. Bye.' Saki waved to everyone.

'Thank you!' called Reiji. His usual buoyant voice rang out – a far cry from how he sounded when the woman had left with those unsettling words.

Saki suddenly turned around at the doorway and spoke to Kazu.

'If Reiko comes by, could you check how she's doing?'

'Sure,' said Kazu with a nod, and began clearing away Saki's cup.

'What's the story with Reiko?' enquired Nanako.

'Oh, this and that,' replied Saki hurriedly, as she rushed out of the door.

DA-DING-DONG

'Saki! Hold on!' Nanako called after her, noticing the photo on the floor by the door. But Saki didn't hear and trotted off briskly. Intending to chase after her to deliver it, she ran over to the register and picked up the photo from the floor. But then, she just stared at it, tilting her head in confusion.

'Huh? . . . Kazu. This . . .' Rather than chase after Saki, she held out the photo for Kazu to see. 'I thought Saki must have dropped it, but I don't think it's hers . . .'

The photo was not of Saki but of a young woman, a man of similar age and a new-born baby. The baby was cradled in the woman's arms. And there was one more person in the photo: it was Yukari Tokita.

Yukari owned the cafe. Nagare, who worked there, was her

son, and Kazu's mother, Kaname Tokita, was her younger sister. Yukari was a free-spirited woman who spontaneously did whatever she wanted. She had the complete opposite personality to Nagare, whose staidness and strong sense of responsibility made him put others first. Two months ago, Yukari had gone to America with an American boy who had visited the cafe. They had gone in search of the boy's father, who had vanished.

With the owner suddenly gone, the only person left to run the cafe was Reiji, who usually only helped out every now and again. Yukari had planned to close the cafe for an extended period until she returned. As she intended to pay Reiji his wages, she couldn't see how closing it for a while would inconvenience anyone. But Reiji hated the idea of freeloading like that.

At the time, Reiji had just been planning a visit to Tokyo, so he dropped by the Funiculi Funicula cafe, run by Nagare, to ask him if he could somehow help to keep the cafe open. Nagare felt like he had a responsibility to make up for his mother's flighty and capricious behaviour, so he agreed to manage the cafe. That was the background in a nutshell to Nagare coming to Hakodate and leaving his daughter, Miki, alone at the Tokyo cafe.

The details, however, were not so simple. Nagare coming on his own would not have solved every problem. Like Funiculi Funicula, the Donna Donna cafe had a seat that allowed customers to slip through time. It was near the entrance and was occupied by the old gentleman in black.

But no coffee poured by Nagare could send visitors to the

past. Time travel was only possible when the coffee was poured by a female member of the Tokita bloodline who was at least seven years of age. Currently, there were four such people: Yukari, Kazu, Nagare's daughter Miki, who he'd left in Tokyo, and Kazu's daughter Sachi. However, when a woman of the Tokita family has a girl, she passes the power to pour the coffee to her daughter and loses it herself.

Yukari had gone to America, Kazu had lost her power to Sachi, and Nagare's daughter Miki had stayed in Tokyo so she would be there when her mother visited from the past. This meant that only Sachi was available to pour the coffee at the Hakodate cafe.

One less than ideal option was for Nagare to go to Hakodate alone and simply run the cafe without anyone to pour the time-travelling coffee. But Sachi, who had just turned seven, announced she wanted to go.

Yet at only seven she couldn't exactly live away from her mother. Kazu had told Nagare she didn't mind if just she and Sachi went to Hakodate. But Nagare couldn't rightly agree to that – he felt obliged to step up as it was his mother who had been so cavalier. Miki didn't mind the idea of her father being gone for a while either.

'Fumiko and Goro are offering to help out so it's no problem. It's just until Grandma Yukari returns, right? I'll manage fine on my own.'

Miki's support tipped the scales, and the matter was decided. Sachi was very enthusiastic about going, and as their stay could possibly last a while, Kazu decided she should transfer schools.

So, the Tokyo cafe was entrusted to Fumiko and Goro,

who had been regulars for over ten years, and Nagare, Kazu and Sachi made the journey to Hakodate. The only worry remaining was the question of when Yukari would return.

Now eyes were locked on Yukari in the photo.

'Yukari is so young. Look how pretty she is! How many decades ago was this photo taken?' Nanako was obviously picturing Yukari's face as she looked when she left for America. She couldn't hide her amazement at seeing a photo of Yukari looking impossibly young. 'This must have belonged to the young woman who was here all morning.'

Kazu nodded. She clearly thought so too.

'Kazu, look. There's some writing on the back.'

'2030-08-27 20:31 . . . ? That's today's date!'

Based on Yukari's youthful appearance, the photo must have been old. But the date written on the back was unmistakably that day.

More perplexing than that was what was written after those numbers.

I'm so glad we met.

Nanako tilted her head in confusion. Beside her, Kazu thought, *That's tonight* . . .

That night . . .

At closing time, there weren't any customers at Donna Donna – only the old gentleman in black seated at the table closest to the entrance and Sachi, who was sitting at the counter reading her books.

'Time to bring in the front signboard, I guess,' suggested Reiji to Kazu after giving all the tables one final wipe.

'Yes, good idea.'

It was seven thirty and completely dark outside. Reiji stepped out to fetch the signboard, causing the bell to emit a subdued ring.

Closing time was normally at six and customers rarely came in after dark because the street was so steep. But in the summer holiday season the cafe closed at eight as young tourists would occasionally wander in even after night had fallen.

There were thirty minutes until closing. The time for last orders had been and gone so Kazu was already getting ready to close.

'Sachi . . .'

Kazu called to Sachi, sitting at the counter reading, but got no response. Kazu expected as much; it happened all the time. Even so, she always made it a point to call Sachi's name at least once. Kazu picked up the bookmark beside Sachi, gently placed it onto the open page she was reading and closed the book.

'Huh?' Sachi seemed to come to her senses the moment the writing was removed from her line of sight. 'What, Mum?'

Sachi spoke as if she had just noticed Kazu was next to her. She obviously hadn't even heard Kazu calling her moments earlier.

'We're closing. Could you go downstairs and run a bath?'

'OK,' she replied. Dismounting from the stool nimbly, she grabbed the book she had been reading and scampered down the stairs next to the entrance.

Their living space was in the cafe's basement. But as the

building was built on the slope of the hill, even the basement had a window that overlooked Hakodate Port. You might even say they lived on the ground floor and the cafe was upstairs. Kazu stood at the register counting the day's takings.

DA-DING-DONG

Kazu looked up at the sound of the bell to see a customer had entered. It was the young woman from earlier in the day.

As I expected.

With last orders already over, normally she would have politely turned a customer away at this time. But there was that photo.

'Hello. Welcome.'

Greeting her in a soft voice, Kazu stared directly into the young woman's eyes. Her name was Yayoi Seto. Earlier today, Kazu had guessed her to be about twenty, the same age as Nanako, but she couldn't be sure. Looking now at her weary expression, Kazu thought she might actually be younger, but aged beyond her years.

Yayoi stood there in silence looking fixedly at Kazu.

'She says she wants to return to the past,' said Reiji coming in with the signboard. Remaining mute, Yayoi glanced around at Reiji, who had become her mouthpiece, and then stared back at Kazu. It was as if her eyes were asking the question, *Is it really true?*

'Do you know the rules?' Kazu enquired, her question providing the answer – *Yes, it's true!* – to the woman's unspoken question.

'Rules?'

Observing Yayoi's reaction, Reiji looked knowingly at Kazu.

It's that type of customer – the one who's come wishing to return to the past without knowing the rules.

'Shall I explain?'

'Of course.'

Having received the go-ahead from Kazu, Reiji pivoted around to face Yayoi. It was apparent that the job of explaining the rules had also fallen to Reiji when Yukari was there. He didn't appear to be at all nervous or flustered.

'Yes, you can go back. You can return to the past but there are rules that you probably won't like.'

'Rules?'

'There are four very important rules. I don't know why you wish to return to the past, but most people give up those plans and leave after hearing these four rules.'

That was not what Yayoi was expecting to hear, and her eyes turned jaded.

'Why?'

Kazu could already tell from the subtle intonations of Yayoi's words that she was from Osaka or that area. She was obviously thinking, *If I never get to go back to the past, why did I come all this way to Hakodate?*

'First, rule number one,' Reiji quickly began his explanation, perhaps sensing her growing agitation. As he spoke, he waved his index finger as if he was an old hand at doing this. 'While you're back in the past, you won't be able to change the present, no matter how hard you try.'

'What?'

Having only heard the first rule, Yayoi was already looking startled. Reiji continued undeterred. 'If you plan to return to the past to correct an earlier action in your life, it will be a wasted effort.'

'What do you mean?'

'Please, listen carefully.'

Yayoi squinted reluctantly and nodded.

'Let's say hypothetically that you've hit hard times right now; maybe you're in debt, or you just lost your job. Or perhaps your boyfriend just broke up with you, or you were conned in some way. Anyway, let's say you're having a hard time.' Reiji was counting the misfortunes with his fingers. 'Even if you hate your present circumstances and you go back to the past to try your hardest to remedy the situation, you won't fix your debt problem, you'll still be jobless, he'll still be your ex-boyfriend or you still will have been swindled. Nothing will change.'

'Why not?'

With emotion creeping into her voice, Yayoi's Osaka accent became more obvious in her response. This time, even Reiji noticed where she was from.

'It's pointless to ask why; it's just the rule.'

'Please give me a proper explanation!' Yayoi insisted. But Reiji simply shrugged. Throwing a lifeline from the register, Kazu explained, 'No one has any idea who decided it or when the rule was decided.' The point she was trying to make was that explanations were meaningless.

'No one?'

'This cafe was established in the late nineteenth century. Even back then you could travel to the past. But no one knows why you can travel to the past, nor does anyone know the reason for all these annoying rules.'

Reiji pulled out a chair from the table nearest to him, twirled it round and sat back in it. 'We don't really know how it started, but apparently, someone delivered a letter while no one was in the cafe, or something.'

'A letter?'

'Yes. It was written in the letter.'

No matter how hard one tries while back in the past, one cannot change the present.

'It's certainly an incredible rule, don't you think? Out of those who want to return to the past, I imagine most of them would be planning to somehow fix the current mess in their life. Yet, however hard they try, they won't be able to change the present. So they can't fix their lives!'

Reiji's eyes were now glistening. He was clearly excitable when it came to perplexing and incredibly mysterious rules. But he was not the one going back in time, and that made his tone irritating.

Her expression cooled. 'What are the others?' she asked in a low voice.

'You really want to know? Most people decide to leave after only hearing the first rule.'

'What are the other rules?' she repeated, visibly agitated.

Reiji squared his shoulders and continued his explanation. 'The second rule. The only people one may meet while back in the past are those who have visited the cafe.'

'What?'

Yayoi's expression was one of obvious disbelief.

But Reiji kept his composure and continued in a business-like fashion. 'This rule is as it says.'

'Why, though?' she asked with her broad accent. Her regional intonation seemed to get stronger the more confused and emotional she became.

'I think you will understand better after hearing the third rule. To return to the past, one must be seated on a certain chair in this cafe. Moreover, while back in the past, one must remain seated and never move from that chair.'

'So clearly, because of that rule . . .'

Though Yayoi desperately wanted to scream out, *But why does that rule exist?* she bit her tongue. She began to realize she would never get a satisfying answer. *Because it's the rule!* When she started to open her mind to the rules, she found that none of them were really that complicated.

So, when Reiji continued, 'Because of the rule that you cannot move from the chair, it's impossible to go outside this cafe to meet anyone. Therefore . . .'

'. . . you can only meet people who have come to the cafe,' Yayoi found herself answering.

'Exactly,' said Reiji, pointing his finger at Yayoi with a grin. *Hardly something to smile about.*

Without words, Yayoi expressed her disdain by looking away.

'Next . . .'

'What? There's still more?'

'The fourth rule . . . There is a time limit.'

'Oh great, there's even a time limit . . .' Yayoi moaned. She closed her eyes and inhaled deeply. It seemed like she was asking herself *Why did I make such a long journey to Hakodate?*

Observing Yayoi in contemplation, Reiji stood up from his chair.

'Oh, the rules are totally annoying. It's not just you. Most who come here to enquire give up and leave after they hear the rules,' he said, bowing his head apologetically.

But as Reiji had not made those rules, his bows and gestures provided little comfort to Yayoi.

This cafe had seen many other customers, like Yayoi, have their hopes dashed after hearing the rules. They had been shocked and were quick to give up. Some never seriously considered a trip to the past. Others angrily proclaimed it was just a hoax and that those annoying rules must be a smokescreen to conceal the lie about travelling back in time. In part, such reactions were a way for those customers to pull out while saving face.

Kazu and Reiji understood that. Whatever customers said to them, they knew people had gone back to the past. Likewise, on this night, even if Yayoi had started accusing them loudly, 'This is just a big fraud!' Kazu would probably just have replied with 'Whatever you say.'

Reiji suddenly recalled an important detail that he had forgotten. As she was leaving the cafe earlier that day, Yayoi had said those words.

. . . *I'd be better off dead than to live alone.*

In the five years since Reiji started at the cafe, many of the customers who enquired about going back in time had been serious. Even still, most had simply left after learning they could not change the present no matter how hard they tried. Reiji had carelessly assumed this was one of those cases. *How could I forget something so important?* He was regretting he hadn't paid closer attention.

Yayoi was standing before him silent and motionless. The only sound was of time tick-tocking away. Through the window with the view of Hakodate Port the dark night was visible. Far away in that darkness was a phantasm of tiny specks of light. What resembled floating lanterns bobbing in the darkness were actually squid boats, illuminated by their closely strung fishing lamps.

'All right. I understand,' said Yayoi, turning her back to Reiji.

Reiji was in no mood to let Yayoi leave, but he had no idea what to say just at that moment.

'Is this you in the photo?' asked Kazu, showing Yayoi the photo picked up from the floor earlier that day. It was of a young man and woman, likely married, holding a baby, and beside them was Yukari Tokita, the cafe's owner. It had to have been the baby Kazu was referring to.

'What?' reacted Yayoi spontaneously. She walked up and snatched the photo from Kazu's hand. 'Yes,' replied Yayoi, looking fiercely at Kazu.

'And they are your parents?'

'They were killed in a car crash when I was too young to remember.'

'I see.'

She wants to go back and meet her dead parents.

Understanding dawned in Reiji's expression. If Yayoi had come to meet her dead parents, she had satisfied the second rule: her parents had obviously visited the cafe. The photo clearly showed them standing in the cafe.

But if she had been thinking of saving her parents from dying in a car crash, that could never happen. The first rule stood in the way of that: she couldn't change the present.

Once, at the Funiculi Funicula cafe in Tokyo, a woman by the name of Hirai travelled back to see her sister, who had been killed in a traffic accident. Hirai had been a cafe regular. So, she went back fully aware that you cannot bend the rules. All Hirai was able to do was thank her sister and promise to reconcile with her parents. Hirai had chosen to go back in time with a full understanding of the rules, but Yayoi had just now become acquainted with them. Before hearing them listed, she was probably thinking that she could save her parents.

Yayoi carefully put the photo away in her bag.

'I'm sorry I wasted your time,' she blurted and headed for the exit.

'Um . . . wait,' Reiji called out to stop her.

'What is it?' Yayoi stopped but did not turn around.

'Well, you came all this way. Why don't you visit your mum and dad?' he suggested. He sounded tentative, probably to avoid being too pushy in light of her inability to change the present. 'They must have been dear to you. If it wasn't for the rule, you'd want to save them, right? So . . .'

'Oh, what do you know!' yelled Yayoi suddenly.

'What?'

She was glaring at Reiji angrily. Overwhelmed by the force of her eyes, he took two steps back.

'I hate people like that!' Yayoi's lips were trembling. But the brunt of her anger was not directed at Reiji.

Kazu stopped what she was working on.

'They gave birth to me, and then they just went and died.'

As if venting pent-up resentment, Yayoi began to tell her story.

'Without my parents, I was passed around my relatives and ended up being bullied at a children's home. They died and left me alone in this world. How can I not resent them for the hardship and loneliness I suffered?' Yayoi pulled out the photo she had just put away in her handbag. 'But look at this photo!' she said, holding it out for Kazu and Reiji to see. 'Look at their happy faces, oblivious to my pain.'

The photo was shaking in her trembling hand.

'Which is why . . .' Yayoi was desperately suppressing her wild emotions, perhaps anger, or sadness – even she might not have known which – but the emotions she was holding back formed into words and left her mouth. 'If I could meet them, I was thinking they could at least hear my complaint.'

'Is that why you wanted to go back to the past?'

'That's what I intended. But I didn't know there were all those annoying rules, and the more rules I heard, it began to sound kind of crazy. What kind of person believes in time travel anyway? They'd have to be a bit funny in the head.'

Yayoi had been about to leave, but Reiji's words seemed to have hit a nerve, unlocking a torrent of emotions she couldn't stop.

'Did you come to meet your dearly loved parents?' she mocked. 'Do you think it's OK to ask such a thing when you've no idea how I've suffered?'

'No, um, that's . . .'

'You say the present doesn't change? That's OK. I don't care. If nothing can change, then that means I can say anything – right? Well then! If I'm told I can return to the past, of course I want to return to the past. I'll happily grab the opportunity to meet the people who left me alone in this world so I can flat out tell them how much I resent them.'

It was certainly true that nothing could be said that would change the present. That was this cafe's golden rule. It wouldn't even change if, say, the future victims of a car crash were told of their fate. Yayoi was defiantly taking advantage of that rule. She stepped forward. 'OK then, take me back to that day – that carefree day when they were getting their photo taken without a thought to my future,' she said, holding out the photo to Kazu.

What have I done?

Reiji's complexion turned pale as a ghost upon realizing he had set off this outburst. Kazu's expression, on the other hand, remained unchanged.

'All right then,' she replied simply.

'Huh?' Reiji exclaimed in surprise.

Reiji rarely encountered a customer who still wanted to return to the past after hearing such rules. But more worrying was Yayoi's motive for doing so – to tell her parents off. Even if her actions couldn't change the present, he could easily imagine how distressing that would be for her parents.

'Is it really OK that she wants to go to vent a grudge?' Reiji whispered close to Kazu's ear. But he had spoken in a silent cafe with only three people present. No matter how softly he spoke, it was inevitable that Yayoi would overhear.

Yayoi glared at Reiji sharply. He quickly looked down.

Kazu turned to him and asked, 'Could you explain to the customer about the man, please?' The man she was referring to was the old gentleman in black seated on the time-travelling chair. Kazu appeared unfazed by any of the drama unfolding. Each customer had a different reason for going back to the past. It was not her place to judge who was right or wrong. Customers were free to do as they wished. The decision to go back, even once they had accepted that it was not possible to change the fate of someone who had died, was left up to them. Going back to complain was a choice Yayoi was free to make. Reiji's uncomfortable feelings were his to deal with.

Although Reiji still felt uneasy, he did as Kazu instructed.

'OK if I continue? It's important that you listen carefully. In order to go back to the past, you will need to sit on a particular chair in this cafe. Currently that chair is occupied by another customer.'

Yayoi looked around the cafe. The only person who fitted the description of *another customer* was the old gentleman in black.

It was the first time she'd noticed him, even though he must have been sitting there the whole time. She hadn't seen him because of his lack of presence. He was completely still, silently reading a book. Her memory felt unreliable, but she had a feeling he also might have been there earlier that day. Now she had finally taken notice of him, something seemed a bit off. It was difficult to pinpoint, and he didn't actually seem out of place in the old-fashioned, retro interior of this cafe, but anyone seeing this old gentleman walking around town would think he looked like he had come from a different time.

For a start, there were his clothes. To the best of Yayoi's

knowledge, the suit he was wearing was none other than a swallowtail coat, so called because the tail of the jacket was forked like a swallow's tail. He was wearing a top hat, despite being inside. Looking at him was like watching a scene from a movie set in the late nineteenth or early twentieth century. Now that he had caught her attention he stood out, but it wasn't strange that Yayoi hadn't noticed him – he really did blend in with the cafe like a part of the decor.

'I assume that's the seat you're referring to . . .' She looked at Reiji, asking with her eyes alone: *If I sit in that seat, I can return to the past?*

'Er, yes.' As Reiji spoke, he felt his reply was unnecessary. Yayoi, not waiting for an answer, was walking over to the old gentleman quietly sitting there.

'Excuse me.'

'There's no point trying to talk to him,' Reiji called after her.

'Why? What do you mean?' Yayoi asked, turning back to Reiji with a puzzled expression.

Reiji inhaled slowly. 'Because he's a ghost,' he replied.

'What?' She couldn't immediately comprehend. 'What?'

'A ghost.'

'A *ghost*?'

'Yes.'

'You're kidding, right?'

'No, it's no joke.'

'He's sitting there. I can clearly see him.'

Yayoi thought a ghost would be transparent, or something that only certain people could see.

'Yes, I know. But he *is* a ghost.'

It was kind of a hard pitch, but Reiji remained adamant.

How am I meant to believe that?

Those words made it to the tip of Yayoi's tongue, but she chose to swallow them. After all, this was a cafe where you could return to the past. She was in this cafe, planning to slip back through time. If she was on board with that – ready to believe in time travel – she realized the absurdity of her struggle to believe in a ghost that she could actually see.

Besides . . . it's difficult to imagine I'd be satisfied by any explanation.

After all, the explanation of the rules had not satisfied her. So she decided to accept what she was being told at face value. To calm herself down, she took a huge breath then exhaled slowly. Her stern expression softened into almost a look of resignation.

'Then what do I do?' she asked meekly.

'Your only option is to wait,' replied Reiji.

'Wait for what?'

'He gets up and goes to the toilet once a day.'

'He goes to the toilet, even though he's a ghost?'

'Yes.'

Yayoi sighed.

Why does a ghost have to go to the toilet?

She realized it was pointless to ask.

'So, I get to sit there during his toilet break?' Yayoi was getting good at choosing the right questions to ask.

'Right.'

'How long will I have to wait?'

'I don't know.'

'So, I just wait around until he goes to the toilet?'

'Yes.'

'I see.' Yayoi walked with exaggerated clatter of her heels to the counter and sat on a stool.

'Perhaps a drink?' suggested Kazu in front of her.

Yayoi took just a moment to consider. 'All right. I'll have a yuzu ginger tea, hot,' she replied.

Although it was summer, the cafe cooled down a little in the evening. Summer in Hakodate didn't always require air conditioning, even in the middle of the day.

'Sure,' said Kazu. But as she started heading towards the kitchen, Reiji interjected.

'I'll do it.'

'But . . .'

It was now a little past eight and Reiji's shift had ended.

'Special circumstances . . .'

He wanted to see how Yayoi's quest would turn out. Looking at Kazu with pleading eyes, he disappeared into the kitchen.

Sitting at the counter, Yayoi's gaze was not on the old gentleman but rather on the view out of the window. After a moment's silence, she suddenly spoke.

'They must have had the choice not to have the baby, right?' She was muttering to herself while mesmerized by the fishing-boat lamps. Her words came out of the blue without any context, but Kazu knew immediately what she was saying.

Earlier in the day, Nagare had spoken of his own wife, Kei, in front of Nanako and everyone else. He told them how Kei had been warned by her doctor, 'If you give birth to this child, it will definitely shorten your life,' but she wanted to have her daughter Miki. Kazu remembered how Yayoi had been there listening to Nagare's account with a grim stare.

Yayoi had viewed that scenario through the lens of her own circumstances. She was saying, *Surely it's better not to have the child if your own life is at stake.*

'Yes, they could have chosen not to.' Kazu did not disagree.

'Well, luckily for her, she grew up in a nice environment. If she were left alone in the world to fend for herself, like I was, I think she would begrudge her mother for making that choice.'

Kei had died soon after giving birth, but her daughter Miki had Nagare. And Kazu, too. There were also cafe regulars who doted on her. Sure, she had lonely moments, but it wasn't as if she had to make her way in the world alone. Someone was always there to support and protect her. Although she missed having a mother, Miki grew up healthy and happy.

Of course Yayoi had no way of knowing that. When her mother came from the past to meet her, Miki had told her, 'Thank you for having me.'

The totally opposite response would have been to ask, 'Why did you have me?' We can never know what would have happened if Miki's environment had been completely different – if after her mother had brought her into this world and died she hadn't had Nagare and Kazu, if there had been no one she could rely on.

'I suppose she might have,' Kazu allowed.

I'd be better off dead than to live alone.

Those had been Yayoi's parting words earlier that day. But

a girl who has lost her parents cannot survive without relying on someone. Perhaps she had never met an adult worthy of her trust.

When Yayoi had lost her parents the first people to take her in were her uncle – her father's brother – and aunt. They of course said they would take care of her, but the timing was unfortunate. Her aunt had just given birth. As it was their first baby, children were new to them. All of a sudden, they had become the parents of a six-year-old girl and a new-born. Their new parenting life was a series of surprises, and they felt unequipped to manage. It brought up feelings other than love and adoration, making them feel guilty. They believed they had to love this child in their care properly, but at times it just felt like a chore.

Looking after our own baby is difficult enough! Why do we have to look after someone else's child?

Children are sensitive to moods in adults, even at an early age, and they can pick up on what's going on. Yayoi responded by behaving in a more reserved way around her aunt, making her aunt feel worse. In the end, her other aunt, her father's sister, took her in.

That aunt had three children. The oldest was in the upper grades of elementary school and the youngest was one year younger than Yayoi, now seven. Her aunt was used to parenting and she had no trouble accepting Yayoi as her own child.

Ironically, that ended up being the problem. From the adults' perspective, Yayoi, who had lost her own parents, deserved equal affection. From her cousins' perspective, Yayoi had just suddenly appeared as an intruder who was stealing their parents' affection. To make matters worse, the more equally their parents treated her, the more retaliatory her cousins became.

They tried to exclude her. They didn't cause physical harm to her, but all three gradually began ignoring her. Except while their parents were looking on, that is. Only then did they pretend they were all close sisters. All other times, they ignored her. Yayoi once again began feeling alienated.

But there was nowhere else for her to go. There was no one she could talk to, and it chipped away at her heart. Her gloomy feelings affected how she thought of her parents, and she came to see them as the real reason she was condemned to such a life.

Isolation.

The wound in Yayoi's heart, chiselled by how she felt during her childhood, warped her personality significantly. To her, the words *to live life alone* were tied to the disparaging notion that nobody needed her.

In other words . . .

She couldn't see the point of living.

By the time she had drunk half of her yuzu ginger tea, the fishing-boat lamps that she had been watching through the window had grown smaller and more distant.

Suddenly, the flap of a book shutting could be heard.

Yayoi turned her head in the direction of the noise to see the old gentleman rising from the chair.

'Err . . .' Yayoi's voice spontaneously leaked from her mouth. Not so much as a hint in the old gentleman's behaviour indicated he had noticed her reaction. He silently slipped out from between the table and chair and began walking to the toilet near the entrance. Of course, there was no sound to his footsteps, either.

Likewise, the toilet door opened quietly, and upon entering, he seemingly disappeared as the door closed without a sound.

Had she not heard the book close, Yayoi probably would not have noticed the empty seat. She slowly stood up from her stool and motioned with her eyes at Kazu. 'Can I do it now?' she whispered, unnecessarily.

'Yes,' Kazu replied, stopping what she was doing.

While feeling her heartbeat speed up ever so slightly, Yayoi closed the distance between her and the chair in a composed, unhurried manner. A *clop . . . clop* could be heard with each step she took. But the old gentleman had made no sound while he had walked to the toilet.

Suddenly, chills ran down her spine as she realized, *He really is a ghost.*

'Call Sachi,' Kazu whispered to Reiji, who was looking on beside her. Sachi was still in the downstairs living space.

Yayoi couldn't understand why they would call the girl, but Reiji seemed to. He replied with a simple, 'Sure,' and hurried down the stairs.

Yayoi's attention was captured by Reiji, and she was startled to find Kazu standing by her side, carrying a tray. She would have given utterance to her surprise but Kazu was already clearing away the old gentleman's coffee cup. After giving the table a wipe, she said, 'Please sit,' offering Yayoi the chair. Not waiting for Yayoi's response, Kazu returned to the counter, carrying the empty cup.

'Er . . . OK,' Yayoi replied, not to anyone particularly, and slid her body in between the table and chair.

When she sat down, she found it was just an ordinary chair. Its seat was firm and upholstered with floral stripes. It did seem old, like an English-style antique. She had been expecting to feel a sudden jolt, like an electric shock. But she felt nothing of the sort. The chair was going to return her to the past, so she thought she would sense a clear sign of its power – whatever that would be. But the anti-climax of nothing happening prompted her to suspect there was nothing magical about it.

As such doubts encircled Yayoi, Kazu called out from behind the counter. 'Do you remember we explained that there is a time limit?'

'Yes.'

'In a moment, my daughter will pour your coffee.'

'What?'

'The time you can spend in the past will begin when she pours the coffee into your cup, and you can stay there for as long as the coffee doesn't get cold.'

Yayoi struggled to understand this unexpected detail.

'Wait a second . . . coffee? Why coffee?' She wanted a satisfying answer. 'And are you saying that your daughter will be pouring the coffee? . . . Why not you? . . . Does it have to be your daughter? . . . One more thing, the time until the coffee gets cold is a bit short, isn't it? . . . Really? . . . That's the time limit? . . . Eh? . . . Huh?' Yayoi rattled off everything going through her mind. In her restlessness, she had completely forgotten a very important thing.

Because that's the rule . . .

Whatever Yayoi asked, it would be met with that simple answer.

One could not in fact return to the past if tea or cocoa were poured instead of coffee. In truth, even Kazu didn't know why it had to be coffee. It was not as if they were using special coffee beans. Any available commercial coffee beans could be used. There were no specific requirements for the tool used for grinding the coffee either. Nor was there a particular brewing method – whether brewed by drip or syphon, it did not matter. However, the kettle, an heirloom made of silver and used for generations, was necessary. The reason why no other kettle could pour a time-travelling brew was also unknown. Yayoi had come this far, so she had little choice but to reluctantly accept the 'because that's the rule' explanation.

'Kazu,' called Reiji, returning from downstairs. 'Sachi will be here soon . . . she's just getting dressed.'

'Thank you, Reiji,' Kazu replied and stood in front of Yayoi, who was hanging her head, dejected by the explanation that wasn't to her liking.

'What?' asked Yayoi, sensing Kazu's gaze.

'There is one final important rule . . .'

'There are still more rules?' she gasped.

Kazu's expression became more serious.

'When you are back in the past, please drink the entire cup of coffee before it gets cold,' she said sternly. Her tone of voice was clearly implying, *You must do it without fail.*

'Before it gets cold?'

'Yes.'

This time, Yayoi did not ask why. She already knew what the answer would be: *Because that's the rule.*

'That's part of the rule, I gather.'

'Yes.'

But this rule was apparently important; she had to *do it without fail.*

'Let's say . . .'. Yayoi still wasn't satisfied. 'Let's say I didn't drink it all?' she asked, genuinely curious what would happen to her if she broke that rule.

'If you don't finish the whole cup . . .'

'If I don't finish the entire cup?'

'Then you will become a ghost and it will be your turn to continue sitting in that chair.'

Although Kazu's expression was unchanged, the words she uttered bore greater weight. The tension in the air was palpable. That must mean that if she didn't drink all the coffee, *she would die.*

But despite the immensity of that risk, this time, Yayoi remained expressionless. 'I see,' she replied simply.

The scuttle of footsteps could be heard ascending the stairs, and Sachi appeared. Behind her, Nagare was slowly following. Sachi was now in a pure white dress, and over it she was wearing a perfectly fitted child-sized aqua-blue apron, just like the one Kazu had been wearing earlier.

'I'm here, Mum.' Sachi's face showed no signs of anxiety or stress. Perhaps because it was clear in her mind what she had to do, or perhaps she was just being her seven-year-old self.

Kazu nodded in response. 'Get ready,' she said, urging her daughter to go to the kitchen.

'Sure.' Sachi disappeared into the kitchen with hurried steps. Nagare followed to help her prepare.

In the meantime, Yayoi was not moving. She was quietly gazing into space as though her mind was elsewhere. Glancing sideways at Yayoi, Reiji walked over to Kazu and whispered in her ear.

'Do you think it's all right?' he asked.

Realizing that Reiji was talking about Yayoi, Kazu did not reply directly but instead fetched the empty cup of yuzu ginger tea Yayoi had drunk.

'Normally when a customer learns of the possibility of becoming a ghost, they are visibly shocked or find themselves in two minds about returning to the past. It's not like the other rules, which don't pose that kind of deterrent to the merits of going to the past.'

Kazu began washing the cup in the small sink behind the counter.

Reiji continued. 'But when she heard that she might end up as a ghost, she seemed totally fine with it . . .'

The only sound quietly reverberating throughout the cafe was water running in the sink.

Reiji lowered his voice further. 'I kind of have a bad feeling about this.'

He had heard Yayoi earlier say, *Better off dead*. It was hard not to be concerned. But Kazu simply turned off the tap and offered no reply.

'Kazu . . .' Nagare called out from the kitchen. At the same time, Sachi appeared. She was carrying a silver tray at about eye level with unsteady hands. On the tray sat a silver kettle and a pure white coffee cup. The empty cup rattled on its saucer as Sachi made her way to Yayoi with Kazu trailing behind.

'Kazu, I . . .' Reiji called anxiously.

Without even turning around, Kazu cut him short with a curt, 'It will be fine,' leaving him no avenue to pursue.

As she was only seven years old, Sachi was unable to balance the tray with one hand and serve Yayoi with her other hand. That was why Kazu was there to help.

Kazu held the tray while Sachi placed the cup in front of Yayoi using two hands.

'Have the rules been explained?' asked Sachi as she reached for the silver kettle. Sachi was unaware of the prior exchange between Kazu and Yayoi. She was asking whether she should explain the rules from the beginning. Despite her seven years, she had a firm grasp of how to do her job.

'We've explained them already,' said Kazu with a gentle smile.

'All right then.' Sachi held the kettle handle with both hands and turned to face Yayoi. 'Are you ready?'

'Yes,' she replied with downcast eyes, as though she was avoiding Sachi's direct gaze.

Both Reiji and Nagare were observing this interaction with troubled expressions. However, the thoughts running through their minds were completely different. Reiji was worried that Yayoi might never return from the past given her current state of mind, while Nagare was concerned with Sachi's coffee-pouring duties. Only Kazu was looking on with a cool and calm expression.

'Well then . . .' Sachi said, turning to Kazu and smiling. 'Before the coffee gets cold.'

She began to pour the coffee slowly into the cup. Although she was holding the kettle handle with both hands, its spout still wobbled a little, indicating that she was finding it heavy. She looked adorable, deeply concentrating on the spout and hoping nothing would spill.

She's so cute.

Even Yayoi was enchanted by her. In that moment, a single wisp of steam rose from the cup. Yayoi's thoughts drifted vaguely as she held the photo in her hand. Suddenly, everything around her began to shimmer and ripple.

'Ah . . .' Yayoi exclaimed, realizing that her body was becoming one with the steam from the coffee. The shimmering and rippling effects were occurring not to her surroundings, but to herself. She felt her body rise, and at the same time the scenery started falling down around her. Inside this flow, she saw scenes of times past in the cafe projected like a kaleidoscope. Day melted into night; night passed into day. What seemed like a long stretch of time cascaded down in moments.

I'm going back in time.

Yayoi gently closed her eyes. She felt no fear. Her motive was clear to her. There was just one thing that was important. How could she bring about a level of suffering greater than she herself had suffered? No matter what she did, her bitter reality in the present would not change. And so, this was reprisal. She had a score to settle with her parents who had left her alone in this world.

Yayoi hated it when parents were invited to visit school and observe their children in class. The frequency of such occasions varied by school, and at the elementary school she attended, such visits were held three times a year. Often, when that time came around, a friend would notice Yayoi's aunt and say, 'She's not your real mum, is she?' One time, she got into a fight with a boy who made such a remark. However, there was something that upset her far more. On days when parents came to visit the classroom, her friends would complain, 'I don't want my parents to come. It's so embarrassing.'

How it pained her to hear those words! She would have done anything to have her parents there, but they had been taken from her and there was nothing she could do to change that. Why did not having parents bring so much hardship and sorrow? She would have to carry that for her entire life.

There is nothing left for me in this life.

Thus, from that moment, Yayoi's heart was skewed by her dark pessimism. When she started grade six, the resentment in her heart led her to act out wildly at home. Her father's sister's family could no longer handle her, and she was moved into a children's home.

After that, her solitude only strengthened its hold. It encrusted her view that no one could understand her feelings and that in the end, she had no choice but to live life alone. And into this shell she had crawled.

In middle school, she began playing truant. On the days she attended, she found herself feeling increasingly irritated by all her friends, who had parents and happy lives. It pained her to hear her friends talking about their parents, and she grew to detest them. It was an agonizing situation.

Naturally, she didn't go to high school like her peers, and instead began working in casual jobs. She also left the children's home. Spending her days hanging out in net cafes and staying there overnight as well, she became a so-called net cafe refugee. In the warmer weather she would even sleep on the streets. She couldn't keep track of the number of times she had been forced to make a bed of the hard pavement while exposed to the elements and crying herself to sleep. She was constantly wondering what she was living for. What was the reason for enduring such hardship?

Even so, dying like this just seemed too pathetic. Eventually the quest to find the cafe where the only remaining photo of her parents was taken became her sole reason for living.

Then six months ago, she came across a photo that had been uploaded to an internet site that showed a recognizable interior of a cafe, on the hillside of Mount Hakodate in Hakodate city. There was an urban legend that at this cafe you could return to the past.

If that is true . . .

Until then, Yayoi had been working just enough to pay for her living expenses. But for six months she worked harder than ever to save up for a plane ticket to Hakodate.

If I could go back to the past, if I could go back and meet my parents . . .

She looked at her happily smiling parents in the photo.

Your child became this unhappy all because of you, because you both died!

She stifled the urge to scream out her anger.

My life is over. There's no going back now.

After she was able to give them a taste of her struggle, just one-tenth, even one-hundredth of her sadness and suffering, she wanted to die.

No way do I want to die before I've done that!

Then today, Yayoi visited the cafe.

She hadn't bought a return ticket.

For a moment, she experienced nothing but blinding light. The sensations in her arms and legs, which up until then were so slight, had now returned. While blocking the light with what she understood was her hand, she slowly opened her eyes. She could see a window that was radiating a brilliant whiteness. No longer could she spot fishing lamps floating on the pitch-black sea. Now she was faced with the serene backdrop of Hakodate Port against a cloudless blue sky, just as it had looked earlier that day.

I've returned to the past, Yayoi realized in a flash. The world had flipped from night to day. The girl called Sachi who had been standing beside her was gone, along with Kazu and the others. In their place sat people she had never laid eyes on before. In addition to two men in their late twenties, there was also a woman in the seat by the window. And smiling behind the counter was the woman in Yayoi's photo, Yukari, who was attending to a small group of people.

Yukari's eyes flitted to Yayoi and with a small nod of acknowledgement, she returned her attention to the conversation at hand.

'Well? You said you had decided on your comedy duo name?'

'It's decided!' replied a chiselled guy wearing silver-rimmed glasses.

'What's the name?'

'PORON DORON,' screamed his taller, slender and shrilly friend.

What?

The name took Yayoi by surprise. She knew of it. PORON DORON were a popular comedy duo who had made a rapid ascent to stardom in recent years. If the men she was looking at formed PORON DORON, then the tall guy must be Hayashida, the funny one, and the bespectacled guy was Todoroki, the straight one. They were popular enough for even Yayoi to have heard of them, often appearing in comedy skits and in TV shows. But the comedy duo Yayoi knew of were not as young as these two. There was no mistaking it, she had travelled to the past.

'PORON DORON . . . ?' Yukari softly repeated the duo's newly decided name.

'What do you think?' Todoroki and Hayashida asked in unison, staring intently at Yukari. They seemed to adore her, looking up to her like she was their big sister. They both waited with bated breath.

'It's a cool name!' exclaimed Yukari. 'It's the best! A winner! I'd give it a gold medal! You guys will absolutely sell!'

The duo's expressions lit up explosively.

'We did it!'

'What a relief!'

'We've been burning the midnight oil to come up with something you'd like.'

'Yeah, yeah.'

Smiling, the two men high-fived happily.

'But it's a good name. Nice and easy to remember. DORON DERON, was it?'

'PORON DORON!'

'Eh? What?'

The name was wrong. While saying it was easy to remember, she couldn't remember it at all.

'You were just saying it was a winner!'

'Sorry, sorry,' Yukari apologized, pressing her palms together.

In response, Todoroki's shoulders heaved with laughter.

'You nearly had us hook, line and sinker, Yukari.'

'You sure did,' said Hayashida, with an exaggerated sigh.

'We should go soon, guys,' said a woman who was quietly observing behind them. She looked much younger than Todoroki and Hayashida, but her calm disposition evoked an air of maturity. Time was pressing because they had a plane to catch.

'Are you tagging along, Setsuko?'

'Yes, of course,' said the woman called Setsuko, with clarity of purpose.

'Good luck, then.'

'It's those suckers who'll need the good luck.'

'Call us suckers why don't you . . .' Todoroki said jokingly with a sigh.

At that moment, Yukari turned to Yayoi.

'You've come from the future, then?' she asked abruptly.

Although it would have been more orthodox to begin with a few pleasantries, Yukari skipped all that. She spoke as if resuming a conversation that had been momentarily interrupted.

'Er, yes,' Yayoi found herself replying.

'Oh . . .' Todoroki and the other two seemed to notice Yayoi's presence for the first time. 'Well, we've got a plane to catch, so . . .' Todoroki said in a hurry as he picked up a large carry-on bag beside him. If Yukari was close to him like a sister, he would definitely be well acquainted with the cafe's rules.

'OK then. Good luck. I'll be cheering for you.'

All three bowed deeply and left the cafe.

DA-DING-DONG

Yukari casually sent off the three, but she probably had Yayoi on her mind. The fact that Yayoi was sitting in that chair meant that she had come to meet someone. And there was limited time.

'They are heading to Tokyo to try to make it as comedians,' she explained to Yayoi, rather than asking, *Who did you come to meet?* 'That's their dream,' she added, as if she was speaking to a cafe regular.

'What's your name?'

'Eh?'

'Your name. You have one, don't you? A name?'

'It's Yayoi.'

'Yayoi?'

'Yes.'

'That's a pretty name,' Yukari said with a praying gesture in front of her chest.

However, praise about her name did not sit well with Yayoi. She averted her eyes, and her face lost all expression.

'What's wrong?'

'I hate it. That name . . .'

'Why? It's lovely.'

'I have a grudge against my parents who gave it to me.'

Yayoi actually said *grudge*. And she was not casually throwing it around. Yet Yukari was not flustered. She leaned over the counter.

'Then I guess you came to unleash your fury onto your parents?' she asked, with a sparkle of deep fascination in her eyes.

Who is this woman!

Yayoi was not liking Yukari's response – not because she accurately guessed Yayoi's true motives but because she was staring at her as if she were some weird novelty. She was unable to hide her discomfort.

'Is that so bad?' Yayoi said defensively. She knew it was pointless to start arguing with someone she had just met, but she couldn't stop herself. Yukari, however, was in no mind to start lecturing Yayoi. She lifted up a clenched fist.

'It's fine to say whatever you like! After all, whatever you say is not going to change the future you came from,' she said with a shrug.

'Who is this woman . . .' Without thinking, Yayoi blurted out what was on her mind. What's more, the people she actually had an axe to grind with were not even there.

Maybe I messed up somehow?

She was thinking about the day she was meant to return to.

Come to think of it . . .

She couldn't recall ever specifically asking how she should return to the day she wanted to return to. She had just held on to the photo, and vaguely wished, *I want to return to the day the photo was taken.*

'Uh-oh . . .'

Yayoi remembered the conversation Nagare and the others were having earlier. When Nagare's wife travelled from the past to the future, she had planned on travelling ten years, but landed up fifteen years in the future due to a mix-up with the years and the time of day. She hadn't grasped the conversation at the time, but now it all made sense, and worse still, it felt like a stab to the heart. *Is that kind of mistake possible?*

Considering the youthful PORON DORON duo, she figured that she had travelled back in time by roughly twenty years. The problem was that there wasn't only the *day*, there was also the *time*.

Yayoi hadn't made any mental image of a specific time. She had only wished to be taken back to the *day* the photo was taken. One day has twenty-four hours, while coffee gets cold in just fifteen minutes. If she couldn't meet her parents within that fifteen-minute window, then it meant she had come back to the past for nothing. If only she knew the exact date and time, like a date written on the back of the photo . . .

Wait a minute! Wait, wait, wait! Yes . . .

Yayoi hurriedly searched inside her handbag, pulled out the photo and looked at it. It was in the photo. The cafe's clock could be seen in the photo. Behind her smiling parents, who were cradling her, and Yukari, stood the large pendulum clock. The time was . . .

One thirty.

Yayoi looked up at the clock. The time was . . .

One twenty-two.

Eight minutes earlier! Eight minutes earlier!

Yayoi placed her hands on the coffee cup to check the temperature.

It wasn't hot.

It wasn't hot but there was still some time before it was cold. She let out a sigh of relief. The people she needed to face must be about to arrive. And sure enough, right then . . .

DA-DING-DONG

The bell rang. Yayoi grew suddenly tense. *Finally, I can meet them.* Just the thought of seeing her parents in the flesh quickened her breath.

Finally, I can meet them?

Did she just think wishfully about the parents she had for years despised?

'Hello, welcome . . . Oh my! Oh, oh, what a surprise! How wonderful!'

Yukari, raising her frenetic voice, welcomed in Miyuki Seto, who was cradling a baby, and her husband, Keiichi. She engulfed Miyuki with a warm hug.

'Congratulations! You checked out of the hospital today, right? You should have said something. I could have come and picked you up . . . Huh? You made a special effort to drop by? Oh, but I'm so glad you did! I couldn't be happier! I couldn't care if the world ended tomorrow, I'm so happy!' Yukari rattled on, over-joyously.

'Oh, Yukari, you are over the top as always,' boomed Kei-ichi, with a broad smile. Miyuki beside him also beamed happily. They were just as they appeared in the photo. The baby in Miyuki's arms was wrapped in a pale blue baby gown.

Miyuki seemed to notice Yayoi staring blankly and she smiled at her with a small nod.

'Ooh, what a cute little thing, is it a girl?' Yukari peered inside the bundle of gown.

'Yes.'

'I wonder who she resembles?' Yukari cast her eyes back and forth between Miyuki and Keiichi.

'She must take after her mum. If she looked like me, she wouldn't be this cute,' Keiichi replied coyly.

'Yes, for sure.'

'Hey! You're not meant to agree with me!'

'Sorry, sorry.'

'Come on . . .'

A harmonious and happy atmosphere filled the cafe.

What is all this?

Anger began building in Yayoi's heart.

How can they seem so happy . . .

Her childhood memories of feeling like she didn't belong anywhere came flooding back.

It's both of your fault for dying on me . . .

Her memories of being ignored by her cousins, of her truancy at middle school, of missing out on the experience of a high-school education, her life working as a casual labourer. They all were racing around inside her head at once.

I struggled with all these worries and inadequacies all by myself . . .

Anger was not the only thing that Yayoi was feeling. She felt a giant chasm between her world and the world the three people in front of her were living in, despite the only two or three metres of separation, one of sorrow and the other of happiness. She felt alienated, enveloped by profound loneliness.

Yayoi was confined to her seat by the rules, and that made her feel even more excluded. Things only went from bad to worse.

Why is it only me who attracts misfortune?

It was challenging just to take in her parents' happy little family. Her shoulders quivered, and from her downcast eyes fell droplets of tears. Simple sadness at her own misery. The loneliness of abandonment had been so tough.

That's it, the coffee can get cold and make me a ghost – bring it on.

Just as that thought occurred . . .

'There was a time when I thought that I'd be better off dead than being alone.'

That tearful female voice flew into Yayoi's ears.

Wha . . . ?

They were exactly the same words that Yayoi had uttered while departing the cafe earlier today. But now, Yayoi was not the one talking.

Who?

Although her question was rhetorical – it could have only been one person.

Surely not . . .

She looked up and saw that now Keiichi was holding the baby while Miyuki was facing Yukari, lowering her head in a deep bow. The voice's owner was Yayoi's mother, Miyuki.

Miyuki lifted her head and continued. 'I don't know how to thank you, Yukari.'

'Thank me?'

'Yes.'

Yayoi had no idea why Miyuki was suddenly saying this. Moments earlier, weren't they all looking so happy? And did not the photo show a happy family that anyone would envy?

What? How can this be?

Yayoi fixed on Miyuki's words.

'My parents disappeared from my life when I was four, and after that, as I was handed around between my relatives, I never felt there was a place for me.'

Huh?

Yayoi couldn't believe her ears, she had absolutely no idea that her mum had been abandoned as a child.

'Oh, how awful.'

'Then, when I left middle school, my uncle and aunt said they didn't want to keep feeding me if I didn't pull my weight. I wasn't allowed to go to high school, so I started working. But I proved to be pretty useless at everything and couldn't escape failure after failure at work . . .'

'Uh-huh.'

'I was bullied by my colleagues, and when their taunts

became unbearable, I quit. My family accused me of not having enough endurance and kicked me out of the house.'

'How terrible.'

'Why did all these horrible things only happen to me? Why were other people living happily while I was unable to get a decent break anywhere I went? It made me so sad, I began to doubt whether there was any value to being alive.'

As Yukari listened to Miyuki, tears began welling up in her eyes.

'During the winter, five years ago . . . on that day when I was standing at the pier thinking of jumping into the water . . . if you hadn't called out to me, Yukari . . .'

'Yes, I remember that day . . .'

'If I had never met you or found this cafe . . .'

'I dragged you up here, didn't I? Yes, I remember.'

'I don't think I would have ever found my happiness.'

'Oh, come now.'

'So, thank you so much,' said Miyuki, deeply lowering her head once more.

Yayoi couldn't believe what she was hearing. It was the first time she'd heard this. Just like her, Miyuki also had been separated from her parents when she was a little girl. She too had started working after middle school. She had been tormented; she had struggled. And she had even wanted to die.

Yet, despite that . . .

She was different from her. While Yayoi was walking through a life of complaints and dissatisfaction, Miyuki was firmly seizing happiness.

What happened? What was different between her and

Miyuki? Yayoi was so engrossed in the ladies' conversation she was barely remembering to breathe.

'Lift your head up,' said Yukari.

Miyuki responded by slowly rising. Yukari was gazing at her, smiling warmly.

'You should be proud of yourself for sticking with it and never giving up. You were impressive in your persistence. It didn't happen by magic! Remember when I called out to you on that day? Your life didn't suddenly transform by itself, did it? None of your problems suddenly fixed themselves, did they? But you looked to the future and persevered. You have what you have today because you never gave up telling yourself that you had to be happy.'

Miyuki had been listening, nodding with agreement at everything Yukari had said. Thick droplets of tears trickled from her eyes.

'So, lift up your head. You can stand proud. Because you seized the happiness you have now.'

'OK,' Miyuki replied and lifted her head and stuck out her chest. Then she let a smile fill her tear-soaked face.

'Yes, yes, that's a nice look. That's what we want to see. It's important to smile.' Yukari also smiled, looking pleased.

'Oh!' Yukari slapped her hand down, looking like she had just remembered something. 'What's the baby's name?'

'Oh, haven't we said?' Miyuki turned and looked at Kei-ichi holding the baby. Miyuki received the baby from Keiichi's arms. Yayoi knew it already without hearing.

'Yayoi,' said Miyuki.

My name.

'Yayoi . . .'

My name, given to me by my mother.

For what seemed like an extended period of silence but was probably just a split second, Yayoi locked eyes with Yukari.

'Oh really? Is your name Yayoi?' she crooned. 'That's a wonderful name, isn't it?' She gently rubbed baby Yayoi's cheek.

Baby Yayoi scrunched up her face and smiled happily.

GO – NG

The pendulum clock in this cafe announced the half-hour with just a single strike of a low-toned bell that resonated lengthily. The time was one thirty. Yayoi checked the clock in the photo.

Keiichi pulled out a camera from his bag. 'Does anyone mind me taking a photo to remember this moment?' he asked with a sniffle.

'Yes, sure. Um . . . let's see . . .'

Yukari took the camera and walked up to Yayoi.

'Huh?'

Caught unaware, Yayoi's eyes widened.

'Could you please take a photo of us?' Yukari asked, passing her the camera.

'Oh! Umm.' When she looked over, Miyuki and Keiichi were watching her eagerly.

'Thank you, we appreciate it.' Miyuki smiled, and bowed her head.

'Well . . . sure, OK.'

Yayoi took Yukari's camera and peered through the viewfinder.

'Uh . . .' she found herself gasping.

It's the same composition . . .

Miyuki, cradling baby Yayoi, was in the middle with Kei-ichi and Yukari flanking her on either side. Behind them was the large pendulum clock showing one thirty and bright light shining in from the window. Before her eyes, the picture began looking very much like the photo she had always and for ever looked at.

She placed her finger on the camera's shutter button.

'I guess I just point and shoot?'

'Yes, that'll be fine,' Yukari replied. Miyuki in the view-finder smiled at Yayoi.

Uh . . .

At that moment, Yayoi noticed something.

Since her parents died, she had looked at this photo and felt estranged, like a bystander, as though she was not included in the scene. But that was incorrect. She had been part of it. There she was snugly in her mum's hands; she was even smiling. That happiness belonged to both of her parents as well as her.

'OK, here we go.'

Her vision was blurring, and she couldn't see.

'Say cheese . . .'

Yayoi silently pressed the button.

'Thank you,' said Miyuki.

'No problem,' responded Yayoi as she averted her gaze. She returned the camera to Yukari without a word.

'You sure you're OK not voicing your complaint?'

whispered Yukari, with a half-teasing expression. Perhaps Yukari had guessed who Yayoi had travelled back in time to meet.

Although feeling a little crushed, she replied, 'Yes, I'm good.' She reached for the coffee cup. It was almost cold.

Perhaps if I too stuck in there and didn't give up on life . . .

She gulped the coffee down in one go.

Her surroundings felt wavy and her body adopted a shimmer. She began to feel dizzy. Her body evaporated into steam and got caught in a whirlpool in the air.

She could tell that Miyuki and the others were looking up at her rising form. She would never meet them again. As her consciousness thinned out, she found herself yelling, 'Mum! Dad!' Maybe her words reached them . . .

The next thing she knew, she was once again gazing at the tiny fishing lamps through the window. From day to night, just like that. The cafe was now cloaked in an orange hue from the lampshade.

'Ahh . . .'

She had returned. Miyuki and the others were no longer in the cafe. In their place was Sachi peering at her with concern. In a wider circle around her stood Kazu and Nagare and Reiji.

It's not a dream . . .

The photo in her hand showed Miyuki's smiling face, which she had seen through the viewfinder.

It wasn't a dream . . .

Overcome with emotion, Yayoi closed her eyes, and her shoulders quivered.

GO — NG

The clock struck its bell to announce eight thirty. Yayoi was suddenly aware that the old gentleman in black had returned from the toilet and was standing next to her.

'Oh . . .' Yayoi hurriedly stood up from the chair to give the old gentleman back his seat.

'If you'll excuse me . . .' The old gentleman nodded his head courteously and slid in between the table and the chair without a sound.

'How was it?' asked Kazu as she weaved around Yayoi to clear away the cup Yayoi had used and serve the old gentleman a new coffee.

'I . . . er . . .' She held up the photo. 'It seems that I wasn't alone,' she replied. Her relieved expression contrasted starkly with her moist pupils.

'Oh, really?' responded Kazu nonchalantly. Reiji, who had been worrying terribly that she would never return, sat down on the nearest chair with a dramatic sigh of relief.

Oblivious to how Reiji was feeling, Yayoi lithely strolled over to the cash register.

'How much?' she asked cheerfully.

But Kazu didn't move.

Kazu was closer to the cash register than Reiji. Normally in such circumstances, she would head to the register, and she ordinarily would have done so today too. But instead,

Kazu remained motionless with no intention of moving from her position in front of the time-travelling chair.

Quick to respond in such moments, Reiji immediately stood up with the full intention of heading towards the cash register. But Kazu waved him to stop.

What is Kazu thinking?

Reiji crooked his neck.

'I think you'll find there is more to come,' said Kazu to Yayoi and she turned back to the old gentleman sitting in the chair.

At that moment . . .

The old gentleman's body suddenly turned to vapour, which rose up into the ceiling as if it were being sucked into an imaginary vortex. Appearing from beneath the steam was a woman wearing a duffel coat covered with dirt. This spectacle of the old gentleman unexpectedly being replaced by this woman in an instant was like an amazing magic trick.

Having become accustomed to such occurrences, Kazu and Nagare were unfazed. Sachi, on the other hand, was bedazzled as if she really had been watching a magic trick. It couldn't have been the first time Reiji had witnessed it, but he could not hold back his wonderment at the timing of it happening immediately after Yayoi had returned from the past.

'What . . . ?' Standing before the cash register, Yayoi stood in blank amazement at the situation before her eyes.

'Where is this . . . ?'

The woman's voice sounded hoarse. As she looked around the cafe, it became clear her weak pallor was not simply from the shock of the moment. Her face was gaunt with bluish lips, and she had no spark in her eyes. In fact, she looked so feeble that left to her own devices her very survival would be in question. Her clothes were covered in dust as if she had fallen countless times and she seemed unsteady on her feet.

'Mum . . .' Yayoi said suddenly.

Though she spoke that word, she couldn't believe it to be real. The woman who had appeared in the chair was her mother, Miyuki. Yet the Miyuki before her eyes was a completely different person than the one she had met back in the past just moments earlier. Miyuki's strong presence had disappeared. She seemed so fragile, like she could vanish in mere seconds.

'Your mum?' Reiji was also struggling to get a handle on the situation.

Only Kazu remained calm. 'Is everything OK?' she asked Miyuki.

The tone of her enquiry was not unlike what she would use on any day to any customer. Miyuki looked up at Kazu with lost-puppy eyes and ever so briefly paused.

'I'm not sure,' she replied.

She was behaving as if even she had no idea what was happening.

'The lady from this cafe called out to me . . . She had me sit in this chair and served me a cup of coffee. Then I got all dizzy . . . and before I knew it . . .'

Miyuki came to be sitting there. She had no clue where she was. Although the cafe looked the same, she was confused as to why the woman who had been standing in front of her was gone and replaced by a bunch of people she had never seen before.

Sensing Miyuki's confusion, Kazu chose a slower, gentler

tone. 'That lady from the cafe, did she explain anything to you?'

Like the rules, for instance.

Kazu was asking about something that only happened moments earlier, but still, Miyuki had to pause before replying.

'She told me to gently close my eyes and visualize the future I wanted to see.' Her speech was disjointed.

'The future you wanted to see?' interjected Nagare.

Everyone there already had gathered that Miyuki had come from the past. But for some reason Nagare reacted when he heard those words: *the future you wanted to see*. They were far too vague for sending someone off to the future. And it was clear that the woman giving those orders was the cafe owner, his mother, Yukari.

Giving slipshod explanations as usual, moaned Nagare inside his head.

That explanation is so messed up, thought Reiji similarly. That had been the reason Reiji began explaining the rules instead of Yukari when he started working here, and it was probably why his explanation of the rules earlier had been so comprehensive and thorough.

'What else?'

'Other than that . . .' In reply to Kazu's question, Miyuki looked down at the coffee cup in front of her. 'She told me to drink all the coffee before it gets cold.'

'Is that all she said?' asked Nagare this time.

'Yes.'

'Unbelievable.' Nagare scratched his head, now speckled with white hairs. *What was she thinking, giving that kind of explanation? It doesn't matter what the circumstances were. To send someone off to the future like that, with such little warning and preparation. It's unbelievable. She was so irresponsible!* As a member of the Tokita family, and thus familiar with Yukari, Nagare was infuriated by her actions. However, it was pointless to get all worked up about it now in front of Miyuki.

Miyuki's face was filled with confusion.

'What is this place?'

Her question was not about her location. She clearly wanted to know what was going on. Kazu understood what she meant. After providing a simple, easy-to-understand explanation that this was a cafe where you could travel forward or back in time, she concluded, 'I think for sure that this place is decades from your present. It must be the future that you wanted to see.'

Leaving it up to Miyuki to believe it or not, Kazu simply told it how it was, with no attempt to choose her words carefully or dress it up.

Though of course, it wasn't something Miyuki could instantly believe.

'Future?' Doubts filled Miyuki's head. *Why did that woman send me to this place?*

Miyuki then noticed a woman staring at her from across the cash register. Miyuki didn't know that woman was her daughter. There was no way she could. But Yayoi recognized Miyuki as her mother. Yet from Miyuki's appearance, it was before she gave birth to her.

Yayoi didn't know how to react. But still, she felt she should initiate the conversation.

'Um, er, I . . .' she began hesitantly with a faint voice.

But she ended there. She didn't know what to say. Should she introduce herself or not? She couldn't decide.

It didn't help that she found it too painful to look directly at Miyuki's miserable appearance. Certainly, she had heard the story while back in the past: how Miyuki's first foray into society had been unsuccessful, how she met with nothing but failure in work, and how she had lost all hope and tried to throw herself into the bay.

But she had not imagined it was as bad as this. Looking at Miyuki in the state she was now, Yayoi couldn't but think her own struggles paled in comparison with what Miyuki had tasted. There was no comparison. Yayoi had the means to save up for the airfare from Osaka to Hakodate, she had enough money for food, and she had enough clothes not to feel embarrassed in front of others.

Compare that with . . .

Her chest felt constricted. Though she wanted to say something, she couldn't find the right words to say.

Yayoi's struggle must have been reflected in her expression as Miyuki called to her across the cash register in a gentle voice, 'Are you all right?'

The moment Yayoi heard those words, she felt a sudden pang of regret.

What kind of idiot daughter was I? Did I seriously want to return to the past to complain? How stupid is that? In the end, I was just thinking about myself. How pathetic, so pathetic . . .

As Yayoi quietly berated herself, Miyuki looked on curiously.

'She is . . .'

An awkward silence was broken by Kazu.

'Your daughter,' she said and slowly departed from Miyuki's side.

Yayoi stayed motionless.

But . . .

She had probably been waiting for someone else to say it. At any rate, she had been utterly incapable of saying it herself. Kazu no doubt perceived the many emotions running through Yayoi's heart.

Yayoi locked eyes with Miyuki. Confounded by Kazu's words, Miyuki stared back at Yayoi.

After a short silence, she whispered, 'My . . . ?'

Tears beaded in Yayoi's eyes. If that could be described as a reply, then she had replied.

'My . . '

Then suddenly Miyuki covered her face with both hands, and her shoulders heaved as she began crying.

'What? How could this be?'

Yayoi found herself running over to Miyuki's chair. Up close, she noticed Miyuki's bony wrists and shabby coat and they pulled at her heartstrings.

'Mu-Mum . . . ? Yayoi called out in a trembling voice.

'I had decided to end it all.'

Yayoi had heard her reason when back in the past. But something drove her to ask anyway. 'Why?'

'Because there was no hope left for me . . '

She had been ready to throw herself into the winter waters of Hakodate Bay. But Yukari just happened to pass at that crucial moment. Instantly recognizing what Miyuki was thinking, she had called out to her. Then she had sat her in the chair . . .

'When the lady told me to visualize a future that I wanted to see . . . I thought I may as well picture a dream that wouldn't come true . . .'

Miyuki slowly raised her head.

'So, I wished to see my own child's happy face . . .'

Listening to Miyuki saying these words, Nagare watched Yayoi.

I see . . . That explains why the timing of when she appeared was today, when her daughter was in the cafe, he mulled in a low mumble, narrowing his eyes.

But Nagare's mind was in turmoil.

This was completely different from their conventional notion of how one travelled to the 'future'. Doubt lingered in his mind. Could you go to the future and meet the very person you wanted to meet so easily?

Yet regardless of his misgivings, what was important right now was the mother and daughter duo before his eyes. With a mighty effort, he suppressed feelings incongruous to him and focused on observing how things unfolded for Yayoi and Miyuki.

Yayoi edged one step closer to Miyuki.

'It's not a dream.'

'. . . ?'

'It's not a dream, Mum. Here in our present, it is the twenty-seventh of August 2030, at eight thirty . . .' Yayoi looked at the clock that had featured in the photo. 'Thirty-one.'

'2030?'

'I turned twenty this year, with thanks to you for giving birth to me . . .'

'I . . . ?'

'I am super, super happy! Look at my trendy clothes. I'm actually living in Osaka. I'm just here in Hakodate for a holiday.'

'Osaka?'

'Yes. It's a great city. Hakodate is nice too, of course. The food is delicious and the people in Osaka are kind and funny. You know, they are always fooling around making everything a joke.'

'Really?'

'Also, I'm getting married next year.'

A lie.

'Married?'

'So, you're not allowed to die!'

No matter how many times Yayoi wiped her tears, they just kept flowing.

'If you die, you'll change history! If you don't give birth to me, then my happiness will have never existed.'

'Huh? But . . . er . . .'

Under the rules, the present reality cannot change.

Reiji was just about to intervene to correct Yayoi's understanding on that point when Kazu placed her hand on him to stop him.

'Let it go,' whispered Nagare.

It was actually the case that under the rules, nothing could change the present reality. Miyuki would not die, she would have a daughter, who would have to live life alone. None of that would change. The reality of being bullied and being tormented by unpleasant thoughts could not be changed.

Yayoi would be born, and this present reality would be waiting.

However, right now, Miyuki had not been so informed. She had no way of knowing the future.

'You see? You have to live . . .'

Although I hated you, although I have been despising you for leaving me on my own, now I'm wishing for your happiness.

And as such, she didn't wish for Miyuki to die.

'Please live, for my sake.'

I'll also try hard.

That was the honest truth.

'What do you say?'

Yayoi smiled at Miyuki in the most wonderful, radiant way. She was no longer the Yayoi Seto who had hated her past and begrudged her mother and father.

Miyuki gave a little nod.

'OK . . .' she replied. She reached out her hands towards Yayoi. 'Let me take a look at my daughter's face . . .'

Yayoi took one, then two steps closer so that Miyuki could cradle her cheeks.

Miyuki used her thumbs to softly wipe away Yayoi's tears.

'I understand now . . .'

'Uh-huh.'

'Your mum's going to stick at it, so you don't have to cry any more.'

'Uh-huh.'

Yayoi wrapped both her hands around Miyuki's hands.

I will remember this comforting warmth for the rest of my life.

She had been told not to cry any more, but the tears didn't

stop streaming from Yayoi's eyes. This time together could never be recreated and would only last so long.

'The coffee will get cold.'

The advice was given by Sachi, who was nestled in Nagare's arms and was now sleepily rubbing her eyes.

'Ah . . .' Yayoi raised her head as if suddenly remembering. 'You have to drink your coffee before it gets cold, right?' She wished that someone would say that wasn't so, but Kazu quietly replied.

'Yes, that's right.' She was confirming that what they were experiencing right now was neither dream nor fantasy.

Yayoi bit her lip. As Miyuki didn't understand the rules very well, Yayoi explained to her that she must finish all her coffee in order for her to safely return to her original time. Miyuki had already heard the same explanation from Yukari. Though she was sad to say goodbye, she quickly obliged.

'Thank you,' said Miyuki and finished the coffee.

'Mum . . .'

'Oh, I almost forgot . . .' Miyuki's body had begun to fade.

'Your name . . .'

'Huh?'

'I never asked it . . .'

'. . . Yayoi.'

'Yayoi . . . ?'

'Yeah.'

Miyuki's body turned into vapour.

'Yayoi . . . what a beautiful name . . .'

'Mum!'

The vapour wisped upwards . . .

'Yayoi, thank you . . .'

. . . and vanished, as if being sucked into the ceiling.

From beneath, the old gentleman in the black suit re-appeared, behaving as if nothing happened.

The cafe was silent but for the billowing breaths of sleeping Sachi.

Having finished the remaining tasks to close up for the night, Reiji emerged from the kitchen ready to go home. Kazu too was removing her apron.

'Thank you, Reiji,' she said in appreciation.

'What for?'

'You pretty much explained all the rules . . .'

'Oh, no problem. When Yukari poured the coffee, I usually did the explaining.'

Miyuki was a good example of why. All that Yukari said to her was, 'picture the future you want to see' and 'drink the coffee before it gets cold'. If that wasn't slipshod, nothing was.

'She must have caused you a lot of trouble,' mused Nagare, lowering his head apologetically.

'In truth, I was at a complete loss when I started here,' reflected Reiji with a wry smile.

Yukari had mostly operated the cafe, with part-time help from Reiji, until Nagare and the others arrived from Tokyo two months ago. Nagare felt obliged to manage the cafe in his mother's absence, because he felt somehow responsible for Yukari's sudden departure to America. Now he was again apologizing for Yukari's free-spirited and spontaneous nature.

'But to be honest, tonight really scared me.'

'Why?' Nagare tilted his head.

'That woman, Yayoi, seemed defeated. Before she went back to the past, she seemed suicidal.'

'Well, now that you mention it . . .'

'And even though she was unperturbed by the possibility of not returning to the present, Kazu was fine with letting her travel back in time.'

'She could have been planning to do so, looking back at it now . . .' mused Nagare.

'It's been quite a few times now that I've explained the rules. But rarely does anyone actually decide to go back. So, I thought that maybe there was a rule that you must never refuse a customer's wish to return to the past.'

'No, I've never heard of such a rule.'

'But if there's not, why . . .'

While listening to this exchange, Kazu had been switching off the cafe lights except the all-night lamps. Everything was left dimly coloured in sepia.

'I could tell from the photo . . .'

Kazu spoke, while looking out of the window at the floating fishing-boat lamps.

'Huh?'

'It was still in beautiful condition.'

'The photo? What do you mean?'

'It had been taken nearly twenty years ago, yet it had been carefully preserved.'

'Oh, I see,' Nagare muttered softly, as if he had understood what she was saying.

'Wait, I don't understand.' Reiji shook his head and blinked in confusion.

'Come on, think about it . . .' Kazu began walking slowing to the cafe entrance. 'If she really hated her parents, don't you think she would have torn it up and thrown it away by now?'

She opened the door.

Hakodate's summer night breeze felt chilly.

II

The Comedian

Summer is fleeting in Hakodate.

Not long after the first leaf or two falls, Mount Hakodate suddenly comes ablaze with the colours of autumn. During this season, a sloping street called Daisan Regalia Rise attracts tourists in droves for its beautifully cobblestoned paving, straddled by the exotic autumn leaves of the roadside mountain ash trees, all of which creates the mood of a faraway land.

Autumn had also arrived in the large window of the Donna Donna cafe, which overlooked Hakodate Port and the vast blue sky. The red and gold foliage spreading across the base of that panorama filtered into the cafe's atmosphere, making it feel quite romantic.

Maybe that was why, seated at the counter, Nanako Matsubara was thinking, *I'm seeing so many couples.*

Today was Sunday. With double the usual number of customers, the cafe was extremely lively. However, as most were tourists, it was an open question as to how many knew this was a cafe where you could return to the past.

Mixed in with the couples was a gangly man in his late forties, whose features were hidden by a hunting cap and sunglasses. Today was the third day in a row he had visited the cafe. Each day he would arrive as soon as the cafe opened and pass his time in there until it closed in the evening. It wouldn't be far off to suggest there was something fishy about him.

Seated in the chair opposite him was Sachi, immersed in her current read: *One Hundred Questions*. Kazu was busy behind the counter and Dr Saki Muraoka was eating lunch next to Nanako. Normally, the sight of Sachi in close proximity to this strange man would have rung alarm bells in the adults, but there was no sense of wariness in anyone. That was because all three women assumed the man was *a customer who had come to visit the past*. Judging by his behaviour, they speculated he was either trying to determine if the rumours about the cafe were true and he could in fact travel to the past, or he already knew the rules and was simply waiting for *the* chair to become free. The cafe saw many dubious customers like him. Most recently, in the last days of summer, a woman seeking her dead parents had first visited the cafe in the morning and then showed up again that evening.

Saki, a psychiatrist at the nearby general hospital, observed the man as she ate her lunch and concluded that he was exhibiting indecisive personality traits. However, his manner didn't suggest he was a dangerous person. Perhaps more perceptive than she was given credit for, Sachi had picked up on this and was conversing with him, reading the questions from *One Hundred Questions* aloud.

'Question fifty-seven.'

'OK.'

Nanako was listening in on this exchange. 'Looks like her new favourite, don't you think?' she said to Kazu. Nanako was talking about *One Hundred Questions*, but given Sachi's behaviour, Kazu realized Sachi had taken a liking to the man in the sunglasses, who was earnestly answering her questions.

'Say you are having an extra-marital affair . . .'

'An extra-marital affair? That sounds like a hardball question.'

Of course, Sachi didn't know what an extra-marital affair was. She was simply enjoying interacting with this new person by way of this book.

'Say you are.'

'OK.' The man in the sunglasses didn't seem to be finding these questions completely without fun.

Sachi continued with her question.

' "If the world were to end tomorrow, which would you do?

' "1. You spend your remaining time with your husband or wife.

' "2. You spend it with the man or woman with whom you are having an extra-marital affair."

'Which one?'

'Hmmm,' mumbled the man, tilting his head. 'If I answer "two", I think it would tarnish my character.'

The man looked over to Nanako and the others. His fear

of being judged harshly based on his selection seemed less to do with Sachi than with the opinions of Nanako and Saki, who were clearly members of Sachi's in-crowd. Depending on the nature of the question, the exchanges often followed the same pattern.

'Number two then, is it?' Nanako asked, quick to sense a teasing opportunity.

'I'm not saying that. I've never had a wife, let alone any affairs.'

'Still single at your age?' quipped Saki. She was always forthright like that.

'Dr Muraoka . . .' Nanako interjected softly, sensing Saki might have sounded rude.

'My fate, I guess . . .' he said.

'But you seem like a nice guy,' she countered.

'I hear that a lot,' he replied.

Saki unabashedly continued her teasing, and the man replied evasively and diplomatically. Losing patience at having lost her new friend's attention, Sachi intervened.

'Which one?' she asked pressingly.

'Oh, sorry . . . umm, well then I choose "one".'

'Dr Saki?'

Sachi wasn't the tiniest bit curious as to why the man chose 'one'. Immediately she turned her interrogation to Saki.

'I choose "two".'

'Oh?'

Saki's response had induced a wide-eyed reaction from Nanako. She hadn't expected Saki to choose 'two'.

'What? Is that so shocking?'

'Oh, er, it was just unexpected, that's all . . .'

'Why?'

'Oh . . . surely . . . you know . . .' Nanako couldn't voice her thoughts. She was in the opposite camp to Saki.

'I think she's calling your character into question.'

The man casually butted in on the conversation while Nanako faltered. He articulated Nanako's thoughts, which left her feeling flustered.

'No . . . I didn't mean that at all . . .' she protested, with a wave of her hand.

'Why did I choose "two", you ask?'

Saki took it upon herself to voice the question Nanako wanted to ask.

'If I didn't choose "two", what sense would it make that I had had an affair?'

She wasn't defending infidelity. She was simply saying that if she had purposely chosen to do something so frowned upon, then she would have chosen her secret lover in a scenario where the world was ending the next day. She wasn't saying that it was the correct thing to do; just that it was her personal view.

But on hearing that, Nanako replied, 'Oh . . . I see.'

'Next question.'

'OK, ready.'

The man replied to Sachi's lively voice.

'Question fifty-eight.'

'OK.'

' "Say you have a secret child . . ." '

'Another thorny question.'

The man scratched his temple.

' "If the world were to end tomorrow, which would you do?

' "1. Because it is your final chance to come clean and get it off your chest, you confess to your husband or wife.

' "2. You keep it secret and stay a deceiver until the end."

'So, which one?'

'Hmmm . . .'

The man folded his arms and once again tilted his head in thought. From the beginning, no question had been straightforward to answer and no question was the same: would he enter a room that would just save one person, would he return something borrowed, would he hold a wedding ceremony, and so forth. The questions were trivial, but most of them dealt with issues that people tended to procrastinate over. By starting each question with the premise that the world would end tomorrow, the book forced its readers to choose one of the two choices: do or do not.

It was like the famous line in Shakespeare's *Hamlet*: 'To be or not to be, that is the question.'

The line was Hamlet's, whose uncle had murdered his father. In the scene, Hamlet ponders taking revenge, anguishing over whether to *do it or not do it*. Overtaken by greed, the uncle had poisoned his own brother, usurped the throne, and made his brother's widow, Hamlet's mother, his consort. It was clear that the uncle in this story was totally evil. And if Hamlet, fully aware of that truth, had not hesitated and had taken his revenge immediately, it would not have caused unhappiness to anyone. Yet Hamlet was lost. What was he to do? Should he believe the words of a ghost? Would that be wrong? Did he really want to run headfirst into a fight? And could he live with himself if he did nothing? In other words, the guts of the story can be found in Hamlet's irresolute character.

While in that lost state of mind, he loses Ophelia, the woman he most dearly loves, he causes the death of innocent bystanders, his friends plot to murder him, and his mother is poisoned. At the end of the story, both Hamlet and his uncle are dead and even the country is overthrown. The play is epically long, lasting over four hours. However, when you unravel the play to get to the heart of the issue, you could say it's about one individual wavering on the question of *to do or not to do*.

Of course, Nanako, Saki, and the man weren't giving any thought to how *One Hundred Questions* successfully pushed the reader to make big fork-in-the-road decisions. They were just playing around with the concept of making one's final choice in the hypothetical scenario of the world ending.

'Indecisiveness is self-destructive,' warned Sachi to the man in sunglasses, who was indecisive like Hamlet. Having read the entire works of Shakespeare, child prodigy Sachi was probably the only one among them who had some inkling that *One Hundred Questions* was more than a simple book for light entertainment.

DA-DING-DONG

The bell rang.

'I'm back.'

Walking through the door was not a customer, but Reiji. He wheeled in a carry-on suitcase. On his shoulder was a backpack and in his hand, a paper bag filled with souvenirs.

'Reiji! Welcome back!' Sachi greeted him.

'Hey, hi Sachi,' greeted Reiji in response, and with that, walked through to the kitchen.

In the kitchen, Nagare said to him, 'You must have just arrived from Tokyo. You could have rested before coming to the cafe.'

'I'm fine. Today's Sunday and it's going to get more crowded.'

Nagare had only arrived in Hakodate two months earlier and had no idea how crowded the cafe became during the autumn-foliage tourist season. Tokyo's Funiculi Funicula was a basement cafe down a narrow side street, so holiday season or not, it was always quiet. Its customers were mostly regulars. And anyway, it only had nine seats – eight, actually, not counting the time-travelling chair.

But in Hakodate, Nagare found himself in peak season. The cafe seated eighteen, including the outside terrace seats. All those seats could be filled, too. He could hardly refuse the offer of one extra pair of hands.

Reiji returned from the kitchen aproned up, carrying two parfaits on a tray.

'Where are the souvenirs?' asked Nanako.

'Let's do that later . . .' Reiji said, as he stepped out to the terrace to serve the parfaits. Even at this time of the year, it was still not too chilly to sit out there around midday. On such a lovely day, the terrace was particularly beautiful, an ideal place to sit while enjoying the colours of autumn. After serving the parfaits, Reiji paused to converse with the customers before returning; he was probably recommending the best sights to see in Hakodate.

'How was the audition?'

'Oh, not bad, they reacted better to my material this time,' replied Reiji proudly to Nanako's question. He was an aspiring comedian, and every now and then he would glimpse an opportunity for his debut and travel to Tokyo for an audition. However, all his attempts to date had fallen short.

Saki, too, knew of his efforts. 'Are you still throwing your money away on trips to Tokyo in the hope of passing an audition?' she muttered with an exasperated sigh.

'I'm not throwing my money away! It's an investment! I'm investing in my future!'

'Isn't it time you let go of that dream? Reiji, face it, you've no talent!'

Even in times like this, Saki didn't mince her words. On the contrary, she dished it out more harshly to those she had known the longest.

But Reiji remained unperturbed. 'That's not true at all.'

'Come on, open your eyes,' Saki implored, implying Reiji's self-appraisal was flying in the face of results.

Nanako chimed in too. 'It's true. You're not that talented.'

'Hey!' reprimanded Reiji, expressing it in his comedic straight-man style as if he was saying, *Don't you go ganging up on me too!*

Nanako hadn't finished. 'But it takes talent not to give up regardless.'

'That doesn't make me feel any better.'

Nanako meant to be encouraging, but her words fell flat.

They had had this conversation many times. Saki was no doubt sincere in her belief that Reiji would be better off forgoing his dream of becoming a comedian. However, Reiji took what she was saying as words in jest. After all, to a man driven by his dreams, such words are like water off a duck's back.

Reiji noticed Sachi was holding *One Hundred Questions*.

'Oh, which question are you up to?'

'Fifty-eight.'

'The secret child one?'

Reiji knew the questions by heart.

Saki's eyes widened. 'You learnt them all?' she shrieked.

'That kind of thing, I can remember after the first reading.'

'Well, I think there's other lines of work besides comedy where that talent would be handy.'

'Enough!'

If Reiji hadn't brought an end to the discussion there and then, Nanako would have added, *For sure!* to cast her vote with Saki.

This exchange between the grownups was of no interest to Sachi.

'Which one?' she asked Reiji.

'Ooh, let me think . . .'

Reiji must have made a decision last time he answered the question. But he put on a show of stewing over the question for Sachi's benefit. He knew that part of the exchange was what Sachi enjoyed most. Just then, Reiji's eyes landed on the man in the sunglasses. At the same time, the man suspiciously covered his face with both hands.

'Mr Hayashida?'

'Ah, er . . .'

'You're Hayashida from the comedy duo PORON DORON!'

'No, I'm just an American shop, you mistakenly entered,' replied the man, and then exclaimed, 'Ah, busted.'

The man's name was Kohta Hayashida. He was a comedian who had enjoyed a rapid ascent to fame over the last few years. His immediate response to Reiji's question was the punchline in a popular PORON DORON skit.

'It's really you! That's the weird incomprehensible nonsense I've grown to love! You've given the game away. You're PORON DORON's . . .' Reiji suddenly dropped his voice. The cafe was full of customers. 'Kohta Hayashida!' he whispered loudly to Nanako and Saki.

Despite Reiji's excitement, the two remained unmoved. Nanako tilted her head in confusion, wondering why 'American shop' featured in the conversation.

To answer her unspoken question, Reiji explained, 'We use the kanji character for "rice" to write "America", right? So, if you saw a sign on a shop with the "rice" and "shop" kanji characters on it, and walked into the shop expecting to buy some rice, but found American goods, it would be a case of mistaken identity, right? He just was trying to tell me . . . anyway it's a pun.'

The selling point of PORON DORON's comedic style was the silliness in telling a pun that no one understood unless the joke was explained to them.

'Ah . . . I see.'

'Now that you mention it, I thought your face looked familiar . . .'

Reiji's explanation had satisfactorily eased both Nanako's and Saki's confusion, but they didn't seem particularly amazed. Perhaps if it had been Todoroki, the other member of the duo, they might have been more enthusiastic. Todoroki was the more popular of the two. However, in Reiji's eyes, both Todoroki and Hayashida were comedians worthy of admiration, and his excitement was brimming.

'Congratulations on winning the Comedian's Grand Prix! I know all about it. Todoroki declared you would win it five years ago. It's really amazing. Oh, could I have your autograph?'

'Um, er . . .'

'Oh, I'm sorry. I got excited. You deserve your privacy. It's actually a dream of mine to become a comedian. Oh wow. I'm thrilled to see you . . .'

Comparing an exuberant Reiji with quiet Nanako and Saki, the difference could not have been starker. Though the tables would probably turn if a heartthrob idol was in their midst.

'But . . .' Nanako suddenly muttered; she seemed to be recalling something. 'After PORON DORON won the Grand Prix, didn't Todoroki suddenly go missing?'

'What's that?' Reiji's reaction was instant.

'Yes,' Hayashida mumbled. His voice sounded broken and weak. The extent of shock in his eyes was hidden behind sunglasses, but none of his earlier jovial mood remained.

Reiji shrank in embarrassment, realizing how inconsiderate his behaviour had been.

Reports that Todoroki of PORON DORON had gone missing made news headlines some weeks earlier. Some articles speculated that money trouble was the most likely reason, and rumours abounded that he had taken the ten-million-yen prize money from the Comedian's Grand Prix and run. No one knew the truth.

'There's a reason you're here, isn't there?'

It was Kazu who asked. No one had thought Hayashida had been coming to the cafe for three days for nothing. His purpose must be to return to the past. It was easy to suppose that it had something to do with the disappearance of his partner.

In a gesture of resignation, Hayashida removed his sunglasses. 'I thought he might come here, so I've been waiting.'

'For that man who's gone missing?'

'Yes,' replied Hayashida to Kazu's question, keeping his gaze downward.

'Why?'

This was Dr Saki Muraoka's question. She was curious what made him think his missing partner would come here.

'To meet Setsuko.'

'And who is she?' asked Saki.

'His wife. She passed away five years ago.'

So, Hayashida had been waiting for the now-missing Todoroki to turn up here to go back to meet his wife Setsuko who had died five years ago. But if that was the case . . .

Does Todoroki also know this cafe's rumour?

Assuming he does, why does Hayashida think Todoroki will come?

Is there a connection between Todoroki's disappearance and his wife who died five years ago?

And why is Hayashida waiting for Todoroki?

Those were the questions hanging over Saki and Reiji at that time. Hayashida then began slowly providing the pieces to the puzzle.

'I grew up with Todoroki and Setsuko in this town. We had been close friends since elementary school.'

The revelation that they were locals made it seem less peculiar that they knew about the time-travelling cafe and its rules. Perhaps they were even familiar faces to Yukari, the cafe's owner currently in America.

He continued his tale.

'Since we were young, Setsuko had always loved comedy. She was the one who inspired us to go to Tokyo to become comedians in the first place.'

Sachi was listening intently to Hayashida's account, sitting perfectly still, just like when she was reading.

'We had zero connections and we really struggled to make ends meet. When we first moved there, all three of us were crammed into this tiny single-room apartment. Todoroki and I would write material and audition, only to get rejected. Our only earnings were minimal performance fees, if you could call them that . . .'

'Excuse me . . .' Hayashida's story was momentarily interrupted by a nearby seated customer. Reiji reluctantly left to attend to him. Hayashida's eyes followed Reiji, but he continued his tale regardless.

'To meet our living expenses, Setsuko worked as a home tutor during the day and as a hostess in Ginza at night. She was running our household and supporting us during that time. She did all that so we . . . well, so that Todoroki could follow a life as a comedian.'

An image of self-sacrificing Setsuko had now been painted. Obviously, she hadn't done it because she was forced to. She must have shared in that hope for success, so that Todoroki – to borrow Hayashida's words – could follow a life as a comedian.

'Todoroki's dream of achieving success as a comedian was one Setsuko shared.'

Of course, becoming a successful comedian must have been Hayashida's dream as well.

'Five years ago, PORON DORON finally clinched a regular slot on late-night TV and Todoroki proposed to Setsuko. We became regulars on that show, but we were still poor, so they forwent the wedding ceremony. I can still remember how happy Setsuko was at the time. But . . .'

Hayashida choked on his words. Everyone knew what happened though he hadn't been able to voice it. Setsuko had died.

'Oh, poor Setsuko, she died too soon . . .'

Nanako averted her eyes.

'Next is the Comedian's Grand Prix . . . Those were Setsuko's final words.'

Reiji had now quietly returned after attending to the customer. While he obviously couldn't know everything that was said, his expression indicated he was still absorbed by the conversation.

'I see . . .' Saki muttered with the air of a knowing doctor.

If the last parting wish of his beloved wife had been for him to win the Comedian's Grand Prix, then upon fulfilling it two months ago, Todoroki would have lost the very thing supporting him. He was enveloped in a deep grief, and the stronger his desire to fulfil her wishes became, the greater his sense of loss must have felt. Such a degree of loss was unfathomable to Hayashida's rapt audience.

'You could call it burnout syndrome . . . up until he had that Comedian's Grand Prix in his hand, he was consumed by a relentless drive to succeed. But when he won it, thereby realizing Setsuko's final dream, he fell apart. Every day, he drowned himself in alcohol.'

Burnout syndrome is considered by some to be a type of depression. But while depression begins with stress or fatigue or a large shock like an accident or a loss, burnout syndrome originates with the thought that all of one's efforts were in vain. It strikes at a time when life is not turning out as expected, despite devotedly pouring one's soul into a certain activity, usually one's work.

However, the term is frequently used in Japan when talking about negative psychological states of elite athletes as an aftermath of major events. Such athletes experience a void-like emptiness in the face of achieving their lifetime's greatest goal, unable to identify the next great challenge.

Hayashida meant the latter when ascribing burnout syndrome to Todoroki. The Comedian's Grand Prix had been

Todoroki's lifetime goal. It meant everything to him. From his standpoint as comedic partner, Hayashida had seen that most clearly. He believed Todoroki's disappearance was due to burnout syndrome, triggered by the Grand Prix victory.

Now Hayashida seemed at a loss. Although he had identified the state that Todoroki was in, he knew of no way of helping. His face was even a little distorted, not by sadness but from a sense of helpless frustration.

'But why did you think that Todoroki would come here now?' Nanako asked.

'That's what I want to know,' chimed in Saki.

As if he had anticipated that question, Hayashida immediately pulled out a postcard from his clutch bag and passed it to Nanako.

'This arrived four days ago.'

The postcard was a photo of a woman against the backdrop of America's vast Monument Valley.

'Ah,' gasped Nanako in surprise.

She showed the postcard to Reiji and the others.

'Yukari?'

Reiji's voice was loud enough to draw stares from the customers in the cafe.

'Er, excuse me.'

'Keep it down, you idiot,' mocked Nanako, smacking the embarrassed Reiji's shoulders.

'Oh, so it is! What a nice smile. Looks like she's having fun, don't you think?' remarked Saki with carefree reflection.

Yukari had gone to America to help a boy find his missing father. In the photo, she appeared to be in high spirits and enjoying her trip based on the way she was happily posing for the camera, with her fingers popped up in the peace sign.

Probably best if we don't show it to Nagare, thought Reiji. Nanako and Saki were thinking along the same lines.

However, it was the message written on the back of the postcard that Hayashida wanted to show them.

Congratulations on being No. 1 in Comedian's
Grand Prix! First prize! What an achievement! I'm
sure Setsuko would be happy for you, too.

Close to two months had passed since the Grand Prix win. She must have somehow found out about it and sent the postcard. It only reached Hayashida four days ago. The manner in which she referred to Setsuko seemed intimate, suggesting Yukari was close friends with all three.

After staring pensively at nowhere in particular, Hayashida abruptly explained. 'As soon as I saw the postcard, I remembered this cafe . . .'

If Hayashida was receiving a postcard sent to his home address, there was no way that there had been no communication between Yukari and the three over the years. It therefore seemed unlikely that the cafe itself was something he could have forgotten. He must have been referring to remembering about the time-travelling aspect of the cafe.

'Todoroki must have received a similar postcard. So, you know . . .'

'You thought that Todoroki would also remember the rumours about the cafe, and come here to meet his deceased wife?' Kazu asked.

'Yes,' Hayashida replied with clear certainty.

He seemed unwavering in his belief that Todoroki would come.

DA-DING-DONG

'Hello, welcome.' Reiji called out instinctively in response to the bell.

Kazu was silently observing the bustling cafe when she recognized the latest customer. 'Reiko?' she muttered.

Reiko Nunokawa visited the cafe on occasion. Her sister had worked part-time at the cafe last year during the height of the tourist season. With a pale complexion and a hint of frailty, Reiko walked in and slowly took in her surroundings, showing no immediate intent to sit down.

'Reiko?' asked Reiji, as he did a double-take. He also knew Reiko well.

Reiko didn't react in the slightest to him calling her name.

'Where's Yukika?' she mumbled weakly.

It was unclear whom she was asking. She wasn't making eye contact with anyone, but was rather gazing vacantly out of the window at the autumn foliage.

'Huh?' Nanako, taken by surprise, turned to Reiji.

Reiji, struggling to come up with an appropriate response, slowly approached her.

'Oh . . . Er . . .' he mumbled, scratching his temple.

Then, suddenly . . .

'She hasn't come yet,' said Kazu.

Reiko turned to Kazu. The awkward silence that followed seemed to last much longer than it actually did.

'I'll come again later then,' she said. Then, slowly retracing her steps, Reiko exited the cafe.

DA-DING . . . DONG . . .

Her appearance and exit were over in a flash, and Reiji and Nanako were left gaping at each other in stunned bewilderment.

Saki was the only one who seemed unsurprised. She stood up and left seven hundred and fifty yen on the counter for lunch.

'Thank you,' she said, and left the shop, as though she was chasing after Reiko.

DA-DING-DONG

'Don't mention it,' Kazu replied as if nothing had happened, nonchalantly observing Saki depart.

'Kazu, I'm pretty certain that two months ago, Yukika . . .' Nanako whispered with a puzzled expression, as her final words failed to carry.

'Yes.'

'But you made it sound like she would be coming later. Why did you lie?' Reiji asked uneasily. He suspected something was amiss based on how Kazu and Saki were acting.

'Let's not discuss that now . . .'

Kazu deflected Reiji's question, returning her attention to Hayashida.

'Oh, excuse me.' Reiji bowed his head in apology to Hayashida.

'No, think nothing of it.'

Hayashida had nothing left to say. He looked relieved, if anything. He had probably been worrying endlessly about the impression he was making. Looking highly suspicious in sunglasses, he had been loitering at the cafe from morning to night. All the while, he had no doubt nursed a cold gut feeling that he would be reported at any time. But now that he had come clean, he felt like a burden had been lifted off his shoulders.

'Well, I think I'll call it a day,' he said and stood up. The midday rush was approaching, and he realized the cafe would soon be very busy.

While standing at the cash register, he presented his card. 'If Todoroki turns up, please contact me before he sits in that chair,' he requested.

Sachi, who had come over to see him off, sadly waved her little hand as she watched him disappear from view.

Soon after Hayashida left, the lunchtime rush began. Nevertheless, the staff had everything under control. Nanako lent them a hand by tending to the cash register, leaving Kazu and Reiji more time to wait on customers. In the kitchen, Nagare was battling it out alone, with Sachi tirelessly cheering him on.

Lunch at a tourist spot is a hurried affair. The excited din lasted for about one and a half hours and later that afternoon only a few couples remained, enjoying a leisurely drink while gazing out of the window. Reiji and Nanako were taking a break at the counter when Kazu spoke.

'According to the doctor . . .' she began. Everyone knew she was referring to Saki. Kazu was continuing the conversation interrupted just before lunch. When Reiko asked about her sister, Kazu informed her that Yukika had not yet arrived at the cafe. But Yukika had died two months ago. Reiji and Nanako knew this and were understandably confused as to why Kazu felt compelled to lie.

Kazu explained, 'Reiko hasn't been able to accept the news of Yukika's death.'

The thought of Reiko wandering around searching for her dead sister touched everyone.

'Oh no, how sad,' said Reiji heavy-heartedly.

Nanako gasped and her hand flew up to cover her mouth. She was lost for words.

'So, Saki asked me to try my best not to contradict what Reiko said.'

Having explained herself, Kazu resumed what she had been doing.

At sundown . . .

The entire cafe interior was tinted orange by the sun setting in the sky. The seasonal boost to customer numbers was generally limited to lunchtime, and by now the cafe was quiet even at this time of the year.

'What?' cried out Nagare, who was taking a break.

He was responding to what Reiji had just said: 'She's your wife! Don't you wish to see her one more time?'

Nagare had no idea how the conversation had led to that.

'The other day, Nanako asked me that very same question . . .'

'Did she? Oh.'

'I can't understand why this is such a hot topic.'

'Well, if you had been in the Tokyo cafe, you could have seen your wife for the first time in fourteen years . . .'

Reiji was referring to the incident in late summer. Nagare's wife Kei had been told by her doctor that she would not survive long after giving birth, and she had travelled from the past to meet her daughter. The timing corresponded exactly with Yukari suddenly taking her trip to America, so Nagare came to Hakodate to fill in as manager and missed Kei. The timing had been dreadful, but considering it was a chance to see his wife after fourteen years, Reiji wanted to ask why Nagare didn't return to Tokyo for that day.

But for Nagare, the answer was simple.

'She didn't come to the future to meet me. She came to meet her daughter, to meet Miki.'

He replied without hesitation. It wasn't a sore point for him. There was nothing to read into. It was as simple as that and Nagare was a man who told it as it was.

'But . . .' Reiji wasn't satisfied.

'What?'

'You had a chance to see her after fourteen years.'

'Well, that I did . . .'

'Didn't you long to meet her?'

'Yeah, but she didn't come to see me, she came to see Miki . . .'

The conversation had come a full circle.

Nagare was expressing his true thoughts. And they were all he had to answer. It perplexed him why Reiji was so obsessed with the notion that he must have longed to see Kei after fourteen years.

'OK then, Nagare, is there anyone you would like to go back to the past to meet?' Reiji was trying a different tack in his line of questioning.

'Anyone that *I* would want to meet?'

'Yes.'

Nagare crossed his arms and further narrowed his naturally narrow eyes as he thought. Then after a while, 'Hmm. No. Nobody,' he muttered.

'But why?'

'Why?'

More to the point, *Why does he want to ask about this?*

Nagare pondered this, tilting his head.

But it was what it was. Although he couldn't understand Reiji's intention, he felt he should try to provide a serious answer.

'Er . . .'

But he didn't know what to say.

'OK, so you're saying that although you have the means to go back in time, you never thought to go back and see your wife?'

'That's what you've been trying to ask?'

'Yes.'

'Well . . . To be honest, I've never thought about it.'

'Really?'

It wasn't the answer Reiji had wanted.

'What's really on your mind?'

This time, it was Reiji who tilted his head and wore a complicated expression on his face. 'In the conversation that took place earlier today, Hayashida said he thought Todoroki would come to the cafe . . .'

'Yeah, OK. What about it?' Nagare hadn't witnessed the conversation first-hand, but he had heard all about it. Yet still, he didn't know what Reiji wanted to say.

'Todoroki wanting to see his dead wife, that's a normal sentiment to have, right?'

'Yeah, of course.'

'But doesn't it seem weird that Hayashida was waiting for Todoroki at the cafe?'

'Huh?' Nagare wasn't getting Reiji's drift. 'He probably just wants to find Todoroki. He's currently missing, right?'

'But doesn't it make you wonder, though?'

'Huh?'

'I mean, why not wait in front of Todoroki's residence if that were the case.'

'Why? Because he's gone missing, I suppose.'

'Why would he think that Todoroki also saw the postcard if he didn't expect him to have visited his home?'

'Ah . . .'

Reiji was continuing to build upon his speculations. He may have been getting just a little intoxicated with his own detective work.

'Perhaps the reporting on his disappearance simply arose because Todoroki abandoned all his work commitments. I mean, is it really possible for someone that well known on television to disappear like that? I'm sure if the police got involved, they would easily find him. So, I just can't understand it.'

'Understand what?'

Already, just like Sherlock Holmes' Watson, Nagare was becoming quite the sounding board for Reiji's deductions.

'Hayashida's behaviour.'

'Hayashida's?'

'I mean think about it. If he just wanted to find Todoroki, then all he had to do was wait outside his home. Why is it so important that he waits at this cafe in Hakodate?'

'Isn't it because he thinks Todoroki will be coming here to return to the past to meet his wife?'

'That doesn't seem like a reason to remain on a stakeout at our cafe for three days.'

'What? Surely you're not suggesting that . . .'

'Exactly.' Reiji's eyes glistened. 'Hayashida must have a reason to stop Todoroki from returning to the past.'

'A reason to stop him? What would that be?'

'That . . .' Reiji paused and Nagare, with bated breath, waited. 'I don't know.'

'Oh. Come on!' Nagare collapsed at the knees in frustration as if hearing the anticlimactic punchline of a long-winded joke.

'Sorry.'

'What are you going on about?'

Reiji began scratching his head.

'OK, say if Kazu were to stop you from returning to the past, why would she do that?'

'Why would Kazu stop me?'

'I mean, hypothetically.'

'I don't think she'd have any reason at all.'

'None?'

'Pretty unlikely. She has never tried to stop a customer from visiting the past. And I can't think why she would want to stop me from doing so.'

'Oh, I see . . .'

A disappointed Reiji felt his shoulders droop. But something about his expression indicated he had more to say. Even Nagare could read it.

'Come on, spit it out. What is it?' Nagare asked, looking him in the eyes.

'I honestly have no idea, but maybe there was something *salacious* going on . . .'

The sudden mention of *salacious* seemed to come from nowhere.

'Huh?'

'What if Todoroki, Hayashida and Setsuko were in some kind of love triangle?'

'Oh . . . surely not.' Nagare swallowed.

'But you can't rule it out?'

Reiji was a little pushy in his tone. And Nagare felt uneasy conversing about secret goings-on. Rubbing his finger on the sweat on his brow was all he could do.

Reiji continued.

'What if Hayashida had a secret that would be in jeopardy if Todoroki went back to see Setsuko?'

'A secret?'

'Yeah.'

'Like what?'

'Like . . .'

DA-DING-DONG

'Hello, wel . . .'

Ah . . .

On seeing the customer who had caused the bell to ring, Reiji gulped. For it was none other than PORON DORON's Todoroki walking in the door.

'. . . come.' Doing his best to conceal his awkwardness, he greeted Todoroki with a salesman's smile.

Todoroki was wearing a grey designer-brand suit. Compared with the tall and gangly Hayashida, he filled out amply in the sideways direction. His hair was unchanged from how it appeared on TV, neat and set in place.

I was expecting an exhausted, defeated man . . .

After hearing Hayashida's account, Reiji had pictured Todoroki with dishevelled hair and shabby clothes at best, and at worst wandering in absolutely sloshed, clasping a 1.8 litre bottle of sake.

Reiji tried ushering him to a table, but Todoroki declined with a gesture of his hand. He made his own way to the counter and sat down on one of the stools.

'Ice-cream soda,' he said to Nagare, who was standing behind the counter.

Ice-cream soda?

This again was not the image of Todoroki that Reiji had in his head.

'Coming right up,' nodded Nagare, glancing at Reiji as he headed towards the kitchen. His eyes seemed to be communicating, *He seems unexpectedly normal . . .*

Evening was slowly encroaching. The sun hadn't fully set but the sky had already turned navy blue.

Crimson autumn leaves and navy-blue sky. Melancholic, but beautiful.

The interior lights in the cafe had been purposely dimmed.

In dribs and drabs, customers settled their bills and left. During this time, Todoroki had been silently gazing out of the window, sipping his ice-cream soda.

'Is Yukari around?' he said, suddenly. The question was directed to Reiji.

'Sorry?'

Reiji was caught off guard by the sudden noise and he hadn't heard Todoroki's question properly.

'Yukari, the owner . . .'

Reiji exchanged looks with Nagare, who had nipped out of the kitchen to check on things.

'Is she taking a day off?'

It seemed that Todoroki, unaware of the situation, had been waiting for Yukari.

Reiki took a step closer to Todoroki.

'Yukari is in America right now.'

'America?' Todoroki's eyes popped wide open in surprise. 'Why is she there?'

Reiji exchanged glances with Nagare again.

'Well, this young guy, after learning of the cafe's rumour, came over from America. Then Yukari announced she was going to try and find his father, who had gone missing . . .'

The boy had thought he could go back to the past to meet his missing father, but as his father had never visited the cafe, he wasn't able to. Seeing the boy bereft of hope and crestfallen, Yukari could not stay out of it.

'And then she went to America?'

'Yes.'

'That's the Yukari I know.' He laughed.

The sight of him roaring heartily was quite different from the image painted in earlier descriptions as a man in hiding.

'Oh, that's a shame. I got this postcard and came to see her . . .'

He held up the same postcard as Hayashida's, the photo of her with America's vast Monument Valley in the background.

'I was thinking she was just on some sightseeing tour. But it's not unlike her. If she sees someone in distress, she can't ignore it and walk on by. It's just in her nature to help . . .'

Todoroki smiled. It was wry, but not bitter. A rather nice smile, in fact.

'Yes, it is,' Reiji agreed.

'So, when is she returning?'

'We have no idea. She occasionally sends a telegram, but that's all.'

'A telegram? They still exist?'

'Yes.'

'OK, I see . . . So I guess it's not possible to go back to the past . . .'

He drew out his final words in disappointment.

Just as predicted, mused Reiji. Todoroki had come to return to the past. But his motives were still unknown. Leaving the postcard on the counter, Todoroki asked for the bill and stood up.

GO − NG

The clock announced five thirty. Todoroki looked at it as he walked towards the cash register.

'Actually, you can go back to the past,' Nagare said to

Todoroki's back. Turning around, Todoroki took in a giant black shadow against the backdrop of illuminated autumn foliage.

'I can go back, you say?' he asked with a hopeful expression.

'You can.'

'There's another member of the Tokita family other than Yukari among you?'

'You seem well versed about the cafe.'

'Yes, this cafe has been part of my life since childhood.'

'Oh, really?'

He didn't ask about such details as who would take Yukari's place in serving the coffee. Todoroki didn't care who it was as long as he could return to the past.

'I'm guessing he hasn't relieved himself today?' he asked turning to look at the old gentleman in black sitting in the chair. The old gentleman unfalteringly continued reading his book.

'No, not yet.'

'Well, all right then.'

Todoroki returned to his stool and ordered another ice-cream soda. A few customers noticing Todoroki approached him. The comedian dutifully indulged his fans, talking to them and even giving his autograph. He didn't seem to mind the attention and jovially gave his best punchlines when so prompted.

Is that really the behaviour of someone in hiding? Reiji wondered.

One customer left, and then another, and finally after the

sun had fully set, only Todoroki remained. Reiji adjusted the lighting to an evening mood.

'Nice,' said Todoroki admiringly.

The outside was lit up and the shade lamps hanging from the ceiling added a gentle flickering of light. In summer, the night vista was the bobbing fishing-boat lamps, and during the autumn viewing season it was the enchanting illumination of glowing autumn foliage. The cafe had a different face for each season. The cafe had only been using this display for a few years, so it was the first time Todoroki saw it.

'Are you going back to meet your deceased wife?' asked Reiji, when he and Todoroki were alone. A momentary flash of confusion passed across Todoroki's face. But it instantly dissipated.

'Why do you know that?' he asked softly in return.

'At lunchtime, Hayashida . . .'

That was all Todoroki needed to hear.

'I see,' he said, cutting Reiji off as if he understood everything. Then he remained silent for a while. After several minutes of looking down silently, Todoroki spoke without looking up.

'What else did he say?' he asked Reiji.

'He said you would probably be coming here to go back in time to meet your deceased wife.'

'Anything else?'

'No, not particularly.'

'Oh, really?'

'Yeah.'

Then Todoroki once again turned silent. For a while,

looking neither at Reiji nor Nagare, he stared vacantly out of the window. Then he spoke again.

'It had been our goal for so long,' he muttered. So soft was his voice, if other customers had still been in the cafe they probably wouldn't have heard him.

'You are referring to the Comedian's Grand Prix, I assume?'

'Yeah,' he replied, longingly toying at the ring on his left ring finger.

'It wasn't so much our dream as it was my wife's . . . Setsuko's . . .'

It was a plain ring without much shine.

'Ever since we won, all I've wanted is to see what joy it would bring to her face. It's made me so restless. My sudden disappearance caused a flurry of rumours. But I was so busy with work, simply going dark on everyone was the only way I could think of getting here . . .' he said with an embarrassed smile, not directed at anyone.

On hearing this, Reiji remembered that earlier he had been speculating about salacious affairs and felt suddenly ashamed. *Love triangle – what was I thinking?* He couldn't even look Nagare in the eye.

'Oh, I see . . . I'm sorry . . .' he said to no one in particular and drooped his head.

Todoroki had no idea why Reiji was apologizing. Nor did he seem to care. He simply gave a cursory nod. Then from his pocket he produced a shiny gold medal. The medal awarded to the winner of the Comedian's Grand Prix.

'After reporting to my wife, I plan on returning to work. So . . .'

He was saying he wanted to return to the past.

'Of course.'

It wasn't Reiji's decision to make; he was simply express-ing in words his wish to facilitate Todoroki's return to the past. Of course, Nagare, who had been listening alongside him, felt the same as Reiji and did not voice an objection.

But why has Hayashida gone to such pains to wait for Todoroki to turn up?

Not every question was answered.

It was probably no big deal, Reiji reasoned to himself. Perhaps it was nothing other than simply hunting Todoroki down. Still feeling ashamed of thinking up a salacious reason, Reiji quashed the doubt that fleetingly entered his mind.

Then, immediately after, 'Hey, I'll text Hayashida,' Todoroki announced. He pulled out his phone, typed a mes-sage and sent it.

Hayashida had asked to be contacted if Todoroki turned up. So surely it wouldn't be a problem if he heard directly from Todoroki.

Things seem to be working out.

Reiji was relieved.

At that moment . . .

Flap.

The sound of a book closing could only mean one thing. The old gentleman in black rose from the chair, tucking the book under his arm. After stretching his back, he pulled in his chin and started walking towards the toilet with a very upright posture. There was silence where footsteps should have been heard. When he reached the door to the toilet, it silently opened by itself and he entered, disappearing into nothingness. The toilet door closed.

Todoroki, Reiji and Nagare gazed fixedly as the scene played out.

The chair was vacant.

If he sat in the chair and received the coffee, Todoroki could return to the past. But for a good while he remained quiet and motionless.

Reiji broke the silence.

'I'll call Sachi,' he told Nagare and started towards the stairs leading to the basement.

Nagare called after him, 'Be sure to call Kazu as well.'

Reiji nodded to himself and disappeared down the stairs.

It was then that Todoroki finally came to his senses. He probably hadn't even noticed Reiji had left the room until then.

Todoroki looked at Nagare, his eyes asking, *Can I sit there?*

'Go for it,' said Nagare.

The tension in Todoroki's face as he headed for the vacant chair reminded Nagare of something.

That something was the hesitation of someone about to meet their . . .

deceased sister,

deceased friend,

deceased mother, or

deceased wife.

The more precious those feelings, the stronger the sense of disorientation. The reason for that was simple. You can reverse time and meet the person you most dearly love, but you cannot reverse death. That was the rule. No matter how hard you try, you cannot change the present.

In Todoroki's case, he was going to report the longed-for

victory of the Comedian's Grand Prix that his wife never got to see while she was alive. He wanted to bring his wife that joy. For Todoroki, this would clearly be that moment of feeling ultimate happiness as he watched his beloved wife Setsuko's joyful face. His news would surely bring great elation for Setsuko, too.

However, the time they would share together would be fleeting – only until the coffee went cold. Then Todoroki would have to come back. If he failed to do so, he would become the ghost sitting in that chair. To journey to the past, it was necessary to sit on the chair with that acceptance. Taking the first step towards that chair was therefore the hardest.

A scuttling of footsteps could be heard, and Reiji appeared.

'They're coming right away.'

Reiji had assumed that Todoroki would already be sitting in the chair. When he saw that Todoroki had not yet risen from his stool at the counter, his eyes wavered about uncomfortably. Maybe moved to action by that look, Todoroki finally stood up and began walking slowly to the chair that would take him back to the past.

Kazu and Sachi appeared from downstairs. Kazu was wearing a long-sleeved denim shirt and black trousers; she was apron-less. Sachi was wearing an aqua-blue apron over an adorable long-sleeved floral dress with a collar and cuff frills.

'I heard your story,' said Kazu to Todoroki, standing in front of the chair.

'So, you're doing the coffee in place of Yukari?'

He felt quite certain that the woman speaking to him would pour the coffee. But when . . .

'No.'

. . . was her reply, he was confounded.

'Oh? So who?'

'My daughter will be pouring the coffee,' Kazu informed him, and looked at Sachi by her side.

'My name is Sachi Tokita,' Sachi said, bowing formally to Todoroki.

For a moment, Todoroki was baffled, but then he remembered: *women of the Tokita family can pour the coffee from the age of seven.* Long ago, Yukari had told him that. *Oh, I see,* he thought. *This child will be pouring the coffee.*

'I look forward to your pouring,' he said with a grin. Sachi smiled back.

'You need to go and prepare,' said Kazu.

'Oh, right,' she replied, and scampered into the kitchen. Nagare naturally followed her.

After watching her disappear into the kitchen, Todoroki finally slid in between the table and chair and sat down. In his childhood, he had often hung out in this cafe, but today marked his first time in the chair. He looked around the cafe from this new viewpoint, taking in the rare experience.

'Did your wife come here often, too?' enquired Kazu. Mentioning Setsuko was her way of telling him that although this was the first time they had met, she was up to date on the situation. Todoroki got the message.

'Yes, I heard that five years ago, just before she died, she came home to Hakodate and visited the cafe to wish Yukari a happy New Year,' he replied. He had a destination date in mind.

'So that day?'

'Yes, that's my plan.'

Setsuko died five years ago. Todoroki apparently knew the exact time she visited the cafe before her death. There was nothing that Kazu needed to explain.

Sachi returned, carrying the tray. For the past few months, Kazu and Reiji had been coaching her on how to carry it. She had been practising daily and was becoming good. But she still looked clumsy while placing the coffee cup in front of Todoroki.

'Have you been told the rules?' she asked politely.

Noticing tension in Sachi's face, Todoroki smiled.

'It's all right. I used to work at the cafe a long time ago. So, don't worry.'

Was that true or not? Not that it mattered; everyone looking on could see he was saying it to reassure the girl before him. Sachi looked round at Kazu, her expression clearly wanting to know if it was OK to continue.

Kazu answered with a smile, and Sachi's expression softened. She was still only seven. It was perfectly natural that she would feel tense.

Sachi placed her hand gently on the silver kettle. 'Well,' she uttered to hold the floor while preparing for what she would tell him next.

'Before the coffee gets cold.'

As those words reverberated throughout the silent cafe, Sachi began pouring coffee into the cup. Slowly and soundlessly, it travelled from the narrow spout of the silver kettle, gradually filling the cup; her countless rehearsals seemed to have paid off.

As he watched the scene in front of him, Todoroki remembered the day he first heard the rumour of this cafe.

'You can travel to the past? No way! Yet you can't change the present? What would be the point of that?' That was the first thing child-him had said. Certainly, when he had spoken those words, he had never contemplated actually going back himself.

Now that I remember, Setsuko was there too. She cried out, 'How wonderful!' and her eyes were glistening . . .

Nostalgia and weirdness became tangled together, and Todoroki found himself chuckling. Directly after that, his body turned into a wisp of steam that rose up and disappeared into the ceiling. It all happened very quickly.

DA-DING-DONG

At that very moment, the bell rang loudly. Hayashida stormed into the cafe and ran up to the chair from where Todoroki had disappeared.

'Gen!' he yelled – Gen was Todoroki's given name.

'Hayashida?'

Reiji's and Sachi's eyes were round with surprise.

'Where is he? Where's Gen?'

'Huh?' Reiji knew Gen was Todoroki's name, but caught in the crossfire of Hayashida's fury, Reiji was flustered.

'If you mean Todoroki, he has just gone to the past to meet his deceased wife . . .'

'Why did you let him do that?' Hayashida demanded, grabbing Reiji by the front of his shirt.

'Mr Ha-Hayashida?'

Sachi was frightened by Hayashida's anger and hid behind Kazu.

Oh . . .

Seeing how frightened she was, Hayashida suddenly shrank and let go of Reiji's shirt. But still, he was unable to stop his racing heart so quickly. He inhaled deeply to take control of his breathing.

Reiji was petrified. 'Wha-what's wrong?' he asked, studying Hayashida's expression.

Hayashida's eyes were fixed on the chair.

'He was just going one-way. He's not returning . . .' he muttered weakly.

'What?' Nagare's narrow eyes opened wide.

Reiji was unable to accept that Todoroki wasn't returning just because Hayashida said so. In his eyes, Todoroki did not seem like a person who had lost the will to live.

But if that was why Hayashida had been waiting at the cafe all this time, all the pieces seemed to fit. He had been intending to stop Todoroki from committing suicide.

'But Todoroki just said he would report his Comedian's Grand Prix victory and come back . . .'

Which he certainly did say. While recalling everything Todoroki had said, Reiji hoped that the notion that Todoroki was not coming back was just excessive worry by Hayashida that he had pent up while waiting. But when Hayashida heard Reiji's words, he sighed heavily.

'He's not coming back.'

'Why do you say that?' Nagare asked.

Hayashida pulled his phone out of his pocket, and after finding what he had been searching for, turned his phone to them.

The screen showed just one line.

Sorry, have to go. Please tie up loose ends.

It must have been the text that Todoroki sent in front of Reiji. The text clearly indicated Todoroki had no intention of returning.

'How could such a thing . . .'

Reiji swallowed his breath and looked at the vacant chair.

Todoroki, Hayashida and Setsuko had all applied for the same school. Hayashida and Setsuko were capable studiers, but Todoroki wasn't. Although he wasn't the smartest, he wasn't entirely inept either. His grades were in the middle-high range, while Hayashida's and Setsuko's were always in the high-high range. In middle school, all three wanted to get into the National Institute of Technology, Hakodate College. As the only national college of technology in the city of Hakodate, it was known as the Tech College. It offered mostly five-year courses in industrial and engineering studies, though mercantile marine studies was five years *and* six months long.

This was before Todoroki and Hayashida decided they wanted to be comedians. Tech College had a comparatively free environment, and its graduate employment rate was high.

Ranked twenty-first among all four hundred and eighty-six high schools in Hokkaido, and first among Hokkaido's fifteen public technical high schools, it had a reputation for being difficult to get in. At the one-on-one interview with their home-class teacher, where students were given honest advice regarding their prospects, Todoroki alone among the three was told in no uncertain terms that he was doomed to fail.

However, Todoroki hated to lose, and he declared, 'I'm the guy who can do anything if I try.'

If all three were going to the same school, Hayashida cool-headedly suggested, 'Perhaps we should adjust to Gen's level.'

But Setsuko was adamant. 'Gen, you've got what it takes to do this!' she said encouragingly.

That decided it. Todoroki started studying like his life depended on it. Setsuko provided motivational support, while Hayashida taught him how to study. For the entire month before the exam, he crammed for more than seven hours every day.

On the day of Tech College's exam, Hakodate received heavy snowfall.

But it was nothing for a snow town like Hakodate. Exams were not cancelled. Silently, snow blanketed down through the still air, cloaking the world in pure white. The three arrived at the exam hall together, everyone fully prepared. Even Todoroki had managed to scrape in with bare passes in mock exams.

'Gen, you would have to be cursed by the gods not to get in with that effort,' said Setsuko, and she gifted him an amulet for exam-passing.

'Don't worry, I've prepared plenty.'

Todoroki puffed his chest out. He had never studied like that in his life. *Perhaps, I might even enjoy studying . . .* he even accidentally thought one day. But in the end, he didn't pass. He alone was unsuccessful in his bid to go to Tech College. He felt bad for disappointing the other two, who had given him so much support, but he had no regrets. He had done his best, which left him with a sense of achievement. Anything he said wouldn't change the fact that he had failed. Setsuko, who should have been happy for passing, was instead crying tears of disappointment.

'I guess this is what happens when you forget to bribe the gods,' Todoroki joked and burst out laughing. Not getting into the national tech college, Todoroki alone went to a public high school.

That spring, on the day of the new-student induction ceremony, Todoroki couldn't believe his eyes. Setsuko was in his class.

'What are you . . .'

Setsuko had rejected Tech College and decided to go to the same public high school as Todoroki. By coincidence, she ended up in the same class as him.

'I guess this is what happens when you give the gods a good bribe,' Setsuko said with a laugh. 'Looks like we'll be together for ever, right?'

Yes, we will be together for ever . . .

Five years earlier

It was the third of January. A snow scene filled the whole vista of the cafe's large window. The sun had just set and the dark blue of the sky reflected on the snow to paint a cobalt-blue world. The streetlights around the Bay Area glowed orange. This was the most beautiful time of the day during Hakodate's winter. Closing time for the cafe was six and given the New Year period, customers had already gone. Only Yukari and Setsuko and the old gentleman were left in the cafe.

It always seemed terribly sudden when someone appeared in the time-travelling chair. As many of the cafe's visitors were tourists, not every customer was in the know about the chair. When the old gentleman sitting close to the entrance suddenly became shrouded in steam and a different person emerged from under it, astonished customers would often cry out, 'What happened?' But Yukari always remained unflustered.

'Did everyone find that entertaining?' she would ask and explain to all the customers around her that they had just witnessed a magic show. A customer might even clap and call it an elaborate performance. Although if someone called for the secret behind the trick, Yukari was careful not to reveal any details . . .

That day as well, the old gentleman was suddenly shrouded in steam. It was, of course, nothing special for Yukari, and even Setsuko had witnessed it a number of times before. But when Setsuko saw who emerged beneath the steam, she shrieked.

'Gen?'

'Hi,' he replied, with a slight raise of his hand.

Setsuko, unable to fathom the reason for Todoroki's sudden appearance, looked to Yukari for help. Yukari promptly altered her expression and walked up to the chair.

'How nice to see you, Gen. Don't you look well! I've been watching you on TV. You're wonderful, wonderful!' she said, holding his hand joyfully.

Todoroki reacted unnaturally. 'Thank you.'

Then a brief conversation unfolded where he provided contrived replies to whatever Yukari said. The interchange between the two continued until Setsuko finally cut in.

'What are you doing here?'

'What?'

'You know what I mean. Have you any idea how startling it is to suddenly see you appear like this?' She puffed out her cheeks crossly.

'I guess, but I couldn't exactly tell you beforehand, could I?'

'Well OK. I suppose not . . .'

What Todoroki said was correct. Left without a comeback, she pouted her lips.

'Did you come from the future?' Yukari enquired.

'Er, yeah.'

'Did something happen?'

Even from this short back and forth, there was something darkly off-putting about his behaviour, something maybe only a close friend could pick up on. Setsuko peered into his face with a worried expression.

From Todoroki's perspective, his wife who should be dead

was right in front of him and he couldn't help feeling disorientated, making it hard to properly look into her face.

Setsuko . . .

If he wasn't careful, he would succumb to the warmth building in his eyes. His tears might reveal that she had died, so he couldn't let them escape.

'Well, lately you've been saying about yourself, "I'm getting so old, I'm getting so old," so . . .' he lied.

'I have?'

'You worried about it so much, I told you I'd go back to the past and see if you've really aged.'

'You came here specially for me?'

'You wouldn't let up. "I've aged, I've aged," you kept saying. What could I do?'

'Huh? Oh really? Well, sorry, I guess . . .'

'Come on, there's no point for you to be apologizing, is there?'

'Oh, I suppose not.'

'Oh my!' he said, and they laughed together. For Setsuko, it was a typical conversation but for Todoroki, it was the first time he had laughed with her for five years. Yukari was studying them closely.

'. . . Well?'

'What?'

'You came here to check, right?'

'Ah, yeah.'

'What's the verdict? So, I have aged then, have I?'

Setsuko leaned forward. 'Have a closer look,' she said, bringing her face very close to his.

'Well?'

'You haven't aged.'

'Truthfully?'

'Yeah.'

Setsuko, as she lived in Todoroki's memories, had died in spring of that year. So of course, she hadn't aged.

'Yes!' she yelled with natural joy.

'And how old am I?'

'What?'

'In how many years will I start worrying that I'm ageing?'

'Five, after five years.'

She crossed her arms and hmmed.

'That would make you forty-three?'

'Yeah.'

'You've aged a bit, I think.'

'Oh, shut up.'

'A-ha-ha.'

This time Setsuko alone laughed joyfully.

That reminded him . . .

Only nine days had passed from the day when, after clinching a regular slot on a late-night TV show, he had proposed; it had been on Christmas Day.

'That was quite the romantic proposal coming from you,' she had teased.

'Oh, shut up,' he had said, as his face flushed crimson.

While smiling with joy, she had told him:

'I am not undecided, but I want to tell Mum and Dad that you proposed before I reply. So just leave it with me, OK?'

Then she immediately booked a flight to Hakodate.

It wasn't until she returned to Tokyo on the fourth of

January that Todoroki received his reply. That day was tomorrow.

'Setsuko, darling . . .'

Yukari, who had been observing their interaction from a distance, called out to Setsuko. At that moment, the smile dropped from Setsuko's face.

'Yes, I know.'

She turned back to Todoroki and bit her lip for a while. Then she expelled a powerful breath.

'So, why did you really come?' she asked him with a sad smile.

Confronted with the sudden question, he blinked. 'What?'

'Stop pretending.'

'I don't know what you mean.'

'You came to bring good news, right?'

She crossed her arms and looked down at Todoroki, smiling smugly.

'Huh?'

'What? Am I wrong?'

'Er, no. Not wrong.'

'OK then, let's hear it.'

The cadence was Setsuko's through and through. She knew Todoroki too well and she understood everything he was thinking. And that had always been the case. Todoroki couldn't run counter to what she said.

Seemingly relenting, he mumbled, 'The Comedian's Grand Prix . . .'

'What? Really?'

'. . . We won.'

'WHOOHOOOOOOOOOOOH!' Setsuko's shriek resounded throughout the room. Luckily there were no other customers at the cafe. But had there been any, she would have reacted no differently.

'Shssshhh.'

'WHOOHOOOOOH!'

'Shsss.'

'WHOOHOOOOOOOH!'

'Shoosh!'

Setsuko was gleeful, running around the room while Todoroki stayed stuck to his chair. If he moved from the chair, he would be forcibly returned to his original time and that would ruin what he wished to do. Setsuko got tired of running and sat in the chair opposite Todoroki, panting from the exertion. She looked directly into his face.

'What?'

'Congratulations.' Her eyes sparkled.

'. . . Ah, yeah.'

'I'm really glad. Nothing beats that for happy news.'

'Now you're exaggerating.'

'I'm serious . . .'

'Oh.'

'Uh-huh.'

Todoroki saw that she was happier than when he proposed. *That's good*, he thought. Meaning . . . *In the end, I got to see her in such a happy state, I have no regrets.*

He smiled for the first time since he arrived in the past.

Now . . .

'I can die in peace.'

The speaker was Setsuko, not Todoroki.

Eh?

He didn't understand what she said. But her meaning was not lost on everyone. Then . . .

'Setsuko, darling . . .' said Yukari abruptly, with tears streaming down her face.

'What are you talking about?'

'Stop pretending I never died.'

Todoroki gulped.

'If I hadn't died, you wouldn't have to be coming back to the past to tell me this news.'

'No.'

'It's OK. You can stop lying.'

'I . . .'

'Look, I already know I'm ill. I've been told I haven't long to live . . .'

'Setsuko . . .'

'I was so happy when you proposed, but I was confused as to what I should do. I couldn't consult with Mum and Dad. It would just upset them to hear about my situation. That's why I turned to Yukari . . .'

Todoroki remembered their aghast expressions the moment he appeared here. While Yukari had started talking with Todoroki after that, Setsuko had kept her back turned to him for a while. It was at that time she realized that she would die and accepted it.

'Thank you. I'm so happy that you came to tell me. I honestly didn't imagine I would ever experience this kind of happiness again.'

'. . . . . .'

'There's no need to cry,' said Setsuko, lovingly wiping away the tears streaming from Todoroki's eyes.

'Hey, the coffee will get cold.'

Todoroki shook his head vehemently.

'What's wrong?'

Setsuko was looking at him with great affection and concern.

'I don't plan on returning.'

'Why would you say that? You just won the Comedian's Grand Prix. You'll be getting lots more work. It's time to put your head down and take advantage of this moment. What was the reason for going to Tokyo if not for now?'

'You were there then . . .' he mumbled. 'I got to see your effervescent face.'

The couple collapsed into their sorrow, their tears falling on the table.

The forty-three-year-old man was reduced to crying with shoulders trembling.

He had thought of giving up on several occasions.

In his mid-thirties, there was a time when they had been frustrated at the pitiful performance fees, and he was always fighting with fellow performers. Every day, he focused on writing material for work. Younger comedians who came on the scene later than PORON DORON got spots on TV before them. Every day was dominated by worry and stress.

Supporting him every one of those days was Setsuko. When Todoroki had a long face, she always encouraged him with a smiling one. And once again, he would remember. *I've been grinding away to make her happy.*

But Setsuko was no longer around.

'I worked so hard at it because you were there.'

So now, it's over . . .

'I know.'

Huh?

'You really love me, don't you?'

As always, she was smiling without a care in the world.

'That's why you kept working at it even after I died?'

'Winning the Comedian's Grand Prix was your dream . . .'

'Sure was.'

'That's why I was just focused on winning. It was all I was living for.'

'And you can keep on fighting, can't you?'

Todoroki shook his head.

'Why not?'

'With you gone, there's nothing to live for.' He started bawling uncontrollably.

But Setsuko just smiled back fondly. He was precious to her.

'But I am still here,' she reminded him gently. 'I'll always be by your side,' she said without hesitation. 'Even though I die, as long as you don't forget me, I'll always be in your heart. The reason you kept working hard even after I died was that I was still in your heart, right?'

In my heart?

'I think it's wonderful if you carry on after I die. It would make me really happy. After all, only you can bring happiness to the dead me.'

. . . to the dead you?

'I love you, Gen, with all my life.'

I . . .

'I won't let you say it's over just because I'm gone.'

. . . thought it was all over when you died.

'So, you can keep on doing it for me, right?'

Todoroki was sobbing like a child.

It doesn't end with death.

Come to think of it, how much of his life had he devoted to fulfilling Setsuko's wishes?

Ten per cent? Perhaps it was only one per cent.

He couldn't say it was with all his life.

He was intending to throw away that life midstream.

He was intending to throw away his life with Setsuko.

That's what she was trying to make him see.

And now he realized.

If he was to make his late wife happy, he would have to fight through this life.

'Now come on, drink up . . .'

Setsuko pushed the coffee closer to him. The coffee would soon get cold.

Todoroki lifted his tear-soaked face and reached for the cup.

'I'll accept your proposal tomorrow. I've been avoiding it, knowing that I'll be leaving you alone by dying early. But now I've said everything I wanted to say.'

'Oh . . .'

She straightened her spine and puffed out her chest.

'You work to make me happy until you die, you understand?'

'OK, I will,' he replied and drank the coffee in a single swig.

'. . . You do that.' Tears trickled from Setsuko's eyes.

Everything in view warped and rippled and the scene around him whirlpooled towards the ceiling. As Todoroki turned into vapour and began rising, Setsuko looked up at him. It was a time of farewell.

'Don't ever forget me until the end of ages.'

'The end of ages?'

'Because my love runs deeper than any grudge.'

'OK, OK.'

'Thanks for coming to see me.'

'Setsuko . . .'

Todoroki was sucked into the ceiling.

'I love you! Gen!'

Setsuko screamed so loud; it ruined her voice.

Then quiet returned to the cafe. After Todoroki disappeared, the old gentleman in the black suit reappeared. He was reading his book as if nothing had ever happened.

Setsuko remembered when she first met Todoroki. It happened not long after a switch-up in classes left her starting grade five in elementary school with unfamiliar classmates. Suddenly the target of bullying, she was called Germy Setsuko by all the boys. Even when she reached out, no one was interested in being her friend. One kid even declared what she touched was dirty. Those days were miserable for young Setsuko.

And then, Todoroki was transferred to Setsuko's class. He

had a gift for making people laugh, and it wasn't long before he was one of the popular kids in the class. But that didn't stop Setsuko from getting bullied.

A boy told Todoroki, 'Careful touching her; you'll catch her germs.'

Setsuko had no comeback. This was how the circle of bullies grew. It was like a process of bonding by making someone the blood sacrifice. Setsuko had accepted her fate and expected this new kid to fall in line. If he went against them, he would be rejected from the circle.

But Todoroki was different.

'Oh, I don't care. If I caught such a cute germ, it might cure my ugliness.' His quip brought immediate laugher. That didn't stop the other kids from bullying Setsuko, but her world vastly changed. It was just Todoroki who felt fondness towards Setsuko. If someone cried out, 'I've got her germs,' and then looked to throw them off to someone else, Todoroki would cry out, 'Give them to me! I'll have them,' bringing everyone to laughter. Setsuko stopped caring if someone picked on her by talking about germs or whatever, because she knew Todoroki would be there to help her. It didn't take long before Setsuko started to like him.

Around that time, the two heard the rumour of the cafe and decided to visit. It was there they met Hayashida, who was in a different class. It was Setsuko's most precious of precious memories.

'. . . Yukari,' she called.

'Hmm?'

'I did a good job then, right?' she uttered, with shoulders trembling. 'I . . .'

'You held it together well'

'. . .'

'You did a great job, right?'

'. . . Uh-huh.'

The illuminated autumn foliage looked exactly like the flames of a fire. After being told by Hayashida that Todoroki was not returning, Reiji's face paled.

'I'm sorry, I never imagined that Todoroki was intending to take a one-way trip to the past.'

Reiji knew it wasn't the kind of problem that could be solved through an apology, but an apology was all he could offer.

'No, I'm at fault too, I should have properly explained.'

The pallor of Reiji's face made it plain to see he was taking it hard. Hayashida too was regretting not being more forthcoming. At any rate, it was not a time to be pointing fingers. Sachi looked up worriedly at Reiji's face.

Such was the heaviness of the atmosphere.

'It will be fine,' said Kazu gently to Reiji. Then she explained what she thought.

'When I heard about the conversation earlier today, I knew that Hayashida had come to prevent Todoroki going back to the past. I also picked up that Todoroki was not intending on returning.'

'What?' exclaimed Reiji.

'Then why did you let him go?' Hayashida asked fiercely in disbelief.

But Kazu was calm, and with a cool expression, she returned his gaze.

'Well, let me ask you something,' she began. 'I assume his wife, Setsuko, also knew the rules?'

'Yes, of course . . .'

'And surely Setsuko was not someone who would allow a person she loved to appear in the chair and wait for the coffee to go cold?'

'Er, that . . .'

Hayashida knew Setsuko would definitely not watch on silently and let Todoroki do such a thing. But he might do the unexpected. What would happen if he took desperate measures, such as purposely spilling the coffee?

'But . . .'

'It will be fine. Look . . .'

As Kazu spoke, she cast her eyes at the chair. Suddenly a plume of steam rose. It dispersed above the chair, like a drop of paint falling into a jar of water, turned into a human figure, and developed into Todoroki.

'Gen, my man!' Hayashida called out.

Instead of replying, Todoroki, with his shoulders shaking, mumbled, 'You idiot, your voice is too loud!'

Shortly, the old gentleman returned from the toilet and stood next to Todoroki. 'Excuse me, I do believe that is my seat,' he announced politely.

'Sorry . . .' Todoroki took a huge sniff to clear his nose and rose from the chair hastily. The old gentleman smiled in a satisfied manner and without making a sound, slid in between the table and the chair.

'Gen!' Hayashida called again.

'I ended up coming back,' Todoroki said, sounding embarrassed.

'Yeah,' Hayashida replied.

'She wouldn't let me say it's over just because she's gone.'

He didn't need to say her name, but it was clear who he was referring to.

'Is that right?' Hayashida's cheeks relaxed.

Well done, Setsuko, was probably what he was thinking.

Todoroki averted his eyes from Hayashida.

'Anyway, you can delete the text I sent earlier,' he said awkwardly.

'You're so erratic.'

'Yeah, sorry.'

Both men then apologized to all the cafe staff for causing such a commotion.

'Please pass on our regards to Yukari when she returns,' they said and left. The world would likely soon see PORON DORON active again.

Kazu, acting as if nothing had happened, let Reiji and Nagare finish tidying up for the night and went back downstairs with Sachi to make dinner.

Reiji's complexion was back to its normal healthy state.

'Kazu always seems to see it right,' Reiji sighed, recalling the events that had just taken place.

With the photo incident at the end of summer, she saw through the emotions of Yayoi who returned to the past. Over the few months that Kazu had been at the cafe, Reiji was impressed by her powers of perception.

Nagare, meanwhile, seemed deep in thought. Reiji noticed that he wasn't progressing with his task at hand. Striking him as kind of strange he asked, 'What's up?'

Nagare turned to Reiji with rather a serious expression. 'I've been giving it a lot of thought . . .' he mumbled, as if he was talking to himself.

'Thought about what?' Reiji cocked his head to one side.

'The reason why I never thought I'd like to see her . . .' He was referring to the conversation that evening that stemmed from Reiji's question. Reiji had asked him, 'Even though you had a chance to meet after fourteen years, didn't you ever think you wanted to meet her?'

Although Reiji had originally asked, he had kind of moved on, considering the conversation ended. But Nagare had been continually mulling over it, having been unable to answer the question.

'It's like Todoroki said just before.'

'Oh? What did he say?'

'She wouldn't let him say it's over just because she's gone,' Nagare muttered.

'Ah, yeah, right.'

'I think that too,' he muttered, 'I've never thought that death was the end.'

He mulled over his words, and then continued. 'She is always inside me. She's living inside us both . . .' Us both, of course, meaning him and his daughter Miki.

GO-NG, GO-NG, GO-NG, GO-NG . . .

With convenient timing, the clock announced six o'clock. The gongs almost sounded like they were proxy to Reiji's feelings as he stood there not knowing how to respond to Nagare's words.

'I feel embarrassed for saying that now,' remarked Nagare after the gongs stopped, closing his eyes more narrowly than usual.

'Yeah,' replied Reiji.

'Pretend I never said it.'

'OK.'

Both Nagare and Reiji resumed cleaning up. The flame-like autumn leaves rustled as if urging them on in their work.

III

The Sister

_____

Please look after the cafe while I'm away.

So stated the letter that Yukari Tokita left for Nagare Tokita before departing for America. She had gone to find the father of a boy who had visited the cafe. Given her propensity for looking after people, she was unable to ignore signs of distress in others.

A few years ago, a woman from Okinawa who was holidaying in Hakodate chanced upon the cafe and learned she could return to the past. She told Yukari she wanted to travel back in time to meet a close childhood friend who had suddenly switched schools. Yukari asked why, and the woman explained that they had fought just before her friend left, and she had long regretted acting so hurtfully towards her.

Alas, she had not yet learned the cafe's rules, specifically, that it was impossible to meet someone who had never visited the cafe. And not only that but she wouldn't be able to move from the chair and her time in the past was limited to how long it took for the coffee to cool. Upon hearing the rules, the woman slumped her shoulders despondently. It was clear that her regret had brought her suffering over many years.

Such conversations were Yukari's weak point. She asked for the woman's contact details; then she later made several trips to Okinawa and used various networks to search for the woman's close friend.

Yukari's strategy was to seek assistance on SNS (social networking services). She herself had little clue about SNS, but through Cafe Funiculi Funicula in Tokyo, she knew Goro Katada, who worked for a world-famous game company, and former systems engineer Fumiko Katada (née Kiyokawa), who, herself, had once long ago returned to the past. Yukari sought their cooperation, including some ideas for a methodology.

One idea was to collaborate with the all-woman YouTuber team Humble Divulgers in finding the missing friend. The Humble Divulgers agreed, and through their viewer reach of more than one million people across a range of ages, they made an appeal on their videos. It actually worked; the friend was tracked down living in Hiroshima, and the two were able to reunite after ten-something years.

Apparently, her friend had also long regretted the fight they had had before she suddenly had to move away for family reasons. But because she had left so abruptly without saying anything, she had imagined there would be hard feelings, and that had always stopped her when she thought of getting back in touch.

*

People's true feelings are not in plain sight. The other person might not be thinking anything, but there is a tendency to just assume what the other is feeling without reaching out and asking. Yukari, on the other hand, was very much the do-and-see type of person, willing to intervene, like in that case, to see for herself what was going on.

Even if the other person cautioned her not to get involved, she would not interpret that to mean that she shouldn't. She had a special persistence. As a general rule, she would only relent after being told not to on three different occasions. It took that long before she understood her interference was unwanted.

The boy from America was no exception. However, this time, she opted for a different approach to her Okinawa effort. She decided to track the boy's missing father by tracing his last known whereabouts. Therefore, just how long *for a while* was, was unknown even for Yukari.

Now, another postcard from Yukari had arrived at the cafe.

It will be a while before I return.

'Is that all it says?' scoffed Dr Saki Muraoka as she peered at the postcard in Nagare's hands. Having finished her shift at the hospital, she had changed back into plain clothes.

'Yep,' Nagare replied neutrally.

'In a sense, it's no surprise, but what do you say to that?'

It was Saki, a non-relative, who seemed more appalled at Yukari's lack of responsibility.

'It's pretty much typical Yukari,' remarked Reiji Ono casually.

Actually, Reiji, through his considerable time at the cafe, had probably witnessed more of Yukari's footloose and fancy-free actions than Nagare, and he spoke as if he was quite used to such things.

It was five o'clock in the evening. Only Saki, one couple, and Reiko Nunokawa were present. Reiko was a regular who had begun showing up because her sister had worked at the cafe over the busy holiday season.

'Dr Muraoka . . .' Reiji asked in a hushed voice.

'What?'

'Why did you decide to bring Reiko here today?'

'Meaning?'

'After all, Yukika . . .'

Reiji trailed off midsentence. Reiko's sister Yukika had been told four months ago she had not long to live, and then she had died. The illness had an obscure name no one had heard of, and the cause was unknown. As cases of that illness were rare in Japan, an established treatment had not been found.

Reiko was unable to sleep from the shock, and on occasion, she would turn up at the cafe looking for Yukika, as if in denial of her death. On several occasions at work, Reiji had seen Reiko in this state.

When Yukika was alive, the two sisters had been close. They were always smiling and in good spirits when he had seen them together. But there was no trace of such joviality in Reiko's face now. Reiji couldn't see how bringing Reiko in her current condition to the cafe could be of any benefit for her. Every time he caught sight of Reiko while going about his work, he felt tremendously uncomfortable. That was how painful it was to see her like that.

Saki simply said, 'Today is different,' and ended the conversation.

Outside, it was getting dark. The lit-up autumn leaves shone bright red. Sitting on the counter stool next to Saki's was Sachi Tokita, holding the book *One Hundred Questions*. Sachi had really taken to the book, and at every opportunity she would ask questions. She had been momentarily interrupted when Nagare and Saki began talking about the postcard Yukari sent.

DA-DING-DONG

'Good evening.'

'It's Nanako!' Sachi's eyes lit up. She was delighted to have one more person to pose her questions to.

'Hello, welcome,' Nagare greeted her.

'Good evening, Sachi,' said Nanako as she sat down on the counter stool next to her. Sachi was now sandwiched by Saki and Nanako. 'Ice-cream soda, please.'

'Righto,' said Nagare, heading to the kitchen.

Nanako Matsubara was Reiji's childhood friend and a student at Hakodate University. Reiji also went to Hakodate University but recently he had been skipping lectures and working nearly every day at the cafe. With his sights set on going to Tokyo to become a comedian, he was focused on saving up for his move to the big city.

After finishing class, Nanako would usually stop by the

university's wind-instrument club, of which she was a member, and then visit the cafe on her way home.

Reiji studied Nanako. 'Hmmm.' Wrinkles formed between his eyebrows.

'Something wrong?' She looked baffled by his behaviour and averted her eyes.

'I'm not sure . . .' He peered at her even more closely.

'What are you doing?'

'There's something about you that's different.' He couldn't quite put his finger on it. 'What is it?' he mused.

'What are you on about?' she countered.

Reiji was perplexed. He felt it in his heart there was something about Nanako he didn't normally see.

But what he as a man could not clearly discern, Saki could see plainly.

'It's her lipstick,' she said.

Even seven-year-old Sachi could have told him that. 'Nanako normally wears a pale mauve, but tonight it's more lustrous,' she pointed out.

'Ohh . . .' Reiji said as he realized.

'Is it a new shade?' Saki asked Nanako.

'Er, maybe.'

It wasn't that Nanako didn't normally wear make-up, but that her new lipstick shade significantly changed her look.

'I thought there was something. The lipstick, huh? Interesting . . .'

Now that Reiji had identified lipstick as the culprit, he turned his attention back to his work behind the counter.

'You look very pretty,' Saki said.

'Thank you.' Nanako couldn't help but smile at Saki's compliment.

'Is there a new guy you like?' Reiji leaned forward from behind the counter.

'Oh? Is that something you care about?'

'I don't care who you go out with, I'm just curious.'

'You don't care about it, but you want to know? What's that meant to mean?'

'It means that it's up to you what kind of guy you would date.'

Nanako tilted her head, trying to work out Reiji's logic. 'If you're curious, doesn't that mean you care?' she remarked.

'No, of course not.'

'How are they different?'

'They are totally different. Who you choose to go out with is up to you. I'm just interested in the kind of personality that your date would have.'

'In other words, you do care.'

'No, caring about something and being curious about something are subtly different.'

'Too subtle for me to understand.'

'Fine, you don't have to.'

Their conversation was getting them nowhere.

Sachi stared blankly while the two continued their back and forth.

'Which question are you up to now?' Nanako had noticed Sachi holding *One Hundred Questions* and quickly changed the conversation.

'Question eighty-six,' Sachi replied happily. It wasn't the kind of book she could read alone. She realized she had more fun when she could ask others questions and listen to their answers. Such opportunities didn't come every day, and she could only get through two or three questions in a day, so roughly two months had passed since she asked her first question.

'Oh, you've nearly made it to the end.'

'Yes, there aren't many questions left.'

'Shall we do some questions, then?'

'Yes, let's!'

For Sachi, who read three regular books in one day, this process of working gradually through one book with Nanako and the others was a uniquely enjoyable experience.

Reiji gave the two a sideways glance, pouted his lips and headed into the kitchen, passing Nagare, who held Nanako's order.

'Here we go, sorry for the wait,' Nagare said, placing an ice-cream soda in front of Nanako.

Above a vivid emerald-green soda water, Nagare had placed a special scoop of ice cream he had made himself from fresh cream, eggs and cane sugar.

'Oh, thank you!'

Nanako's eyes sparkled as she picked up the straw. Nagare's trademark ice-cream soda had become her favourite.

What If The World Were Ending Tomorrow? One Hundred Questions

As Nanako savoured her soda, Sachi began reading the question out loud.

' "Question eighty-seven.

' "You have a child who has just turned ten years old." '

'Sounds like another tough question,' remarked Saki, knitting her brow wryly.

'Ten years old?'

This was Nanako. Sachi nodded slightly to confirm.

'That's rather a borderline age.'

What Nanako meant by *borderline* was that it was an age where a child was still very much a child but now able to understand what adults were talking about. At age ten, a child is a technological expert, so it is no longer possible to explain things in a half-hearted manner. 'OK,' Nanako said, indicating for Sachi to continue.

'"If the world were to end tomorrow, which would you do?

'"1. Keep quiet about it because they wouldn't properly understand.

'"2. Tell the truth because you will feel guilty keeping quiet."'

As soon as Nanako had heard the entire question, she replied without hesitation: 'One.'

'You wouldn't tell them?' Saki asked.

'Ten years old, right? No, I wouldn't. Telling them would only frighten them, which would be pointless.'

'Oh, OK.'

'Would you tell them, Dr Saki?'

'Gosh, the child is only ten, right?'

Saki looked up at the ceiling, and pondered for a while muttering to herself, 'Would I say anything? . . . I probably wouldn't.'

'You wouldn't say anything, right?'

'OK, Nanako, if you were ten, would you want to be told?'

'Me?'

'Would you want to know? Or wouldn't you?'

'Let's see.' This time, Nanako gazed up at the ceiling.

Sachi's eyes sparkled, transfixed by the exchange between the two.

'Maybe I'd want to know.'

'Aren't you being hypocritical then?'

'I'd want to know if it were me. But if it were my own child, I wouldn't want to tell them.'

'Why?'

'I wouldn't mind if I were sad, but I wouldn't want to see my own child sad, I guess.'

'I see,' Saki replied with an understanding nod. There was certainly contradiction in Nanako's thinking, but her 'it is what it is' reasoning was convincing.

'How about you, Uncle Nagare?'

'Err, I think maybe two?'

'Why?'

'Well, besides feeling guilty, I wouldn't be able to hide it.'

His reply prompted Nanako to remark, 'I can imagine. You'd be a hopeless liar.'

'Anyone would be like, "What are you hiding?" and Nagare would come clean right away,' Saki added.

'Sounds about right,' agreed Nagare, scratching her head.

Reiko, seated by the window, had been staring blankly at everyone in conversation.

The pendulum wall clock hammered its gong to announce it was half-past five. The couple, perhaps prompted by the gong, stood up from their chairs, and Reiji made his way to the cash register. Footsteps could be heard approaching, and Kazu Tokita appeared.

'Sachi,' Kazu called.

'What?'

'Dinner's ready.'

'OK.'

Sachi flapped shut *One Hundred Questions*.

'OK, we'll continue this another time,' said Nanako.

'Yes,' Sachi replied, and leaving the book on the counter, she disappeared downstairs. Kazu caught Nagare's eyes and indicated towards Reiko, as if to say: *Please take care of what comes after*. Then she followed Sachi down the stairs.

DA-DING-DONG

The couple had paid and left the cafe.

Apart from Nanako and Saki, the only remaining customer was Reiko.

'Oh, I almost forgot,' said Reiji suddenly. 'Saki, I've written some new material for the next audition. Do you mind having a look and telling me what you think?'

It was something Reiji occasionally asked regulars he was friendly with. His dream was to audition at one of the big entertainment agencies and begin a career as a comedian.

Just several days ago, he got a sudden surge of motivation after finding out that Todoroki and Hayashida of the comedy duo PORON DORON, who appeared regularly on TV, were originally from Hakodate and had once been regulars at this cafe.

Addressing his gung-ho dream with candour, Saki responded flatly, 'You're not funny.' She elaborated further: 'Your jokes suck, timing's terrible. I mean, it's hard to know when I'm meant to laugh. You're making a big mistake pursuing a career in comedy. You really should give it up.'

It was a terrible thing to say.

'Sa-Saki that's a bit too harsh, don't you think?' said Nagare. He was probably about to continue with something about hurting Reiji's feelings. Reiji, however, seemed completely fine with it.

'No, that's simply not true!' he contended with a curt smile, not in the least disheartened. He was a young man with a dream he kept firmly believing in no matter what anyone said.

'Look, I'm telling you out of kindness. One day you'll be wanting to take it all back, and then what? It'll be too late for regrets.'

'It will never be like that because I will never regret it.'

Saki sighed. It was like water off a duck's back, or pee off a frog's face!

'You can try it out on me, if you like?' suggested Nanako.

'No, I don't think so.'

'Why not?'

'Your opinions aren't of any help.'

Reiji was afraid that Nanako would be too soft on him because of their friendship.

'Well, how about you take my opinions on board?' interjected Saki.

Reiji didn't seem to be listening.

'Righto!' he said after an energetic suck of air, and nonchalantly strolled into the kitchen towards his locker.

'Reiji?' Nagare peered into the kitchen.

'?'

Nanako and Nagare exchanged a puzzled look.

After a while, Reiji returned with his joke journal and a large bag.

'Nagare, do you mind handling the rest?'

'Huh? Oh, OK I suppose.'

At this time of the year, the cafe closed at six. The half-past five gong had rung, meaning last orders had finished. *The rest* referred to closing up.

'Where are you going?' a curious Nanako asked Reiji, who had somewhere so urgent to go to, he was leaving mid-shift.

'I'm about to stage a guerrilla live street performance.'

'Now? It will be completely dark outside.'

'Down near Kanemori Hall, there's the hamburger restaurant Lucky Pierrot and there are sure to be tourists still wandering around!'

Kanemori Hall was plumb in the centre of the touristy Bay Area at one end of the red-brick warehouses skirting the waterfront. It was used for concerts, plays and various events. Sandwiching the hall were brick shopping malls and restaurants, and as Reiji said, even at that time of the day, the street outside was a well-lit pedestrian thoroughfare.

The weather, however, was looking ominous. A little earlier, distant thunder had rumbled. Not that any amount of rain, wind or lightning would have deterred Reiji at this moment. 'See you guys!' Unable to contain his restlessness, he abruptly left the cafe.

DA-DING-DONG

'Reiji!'

Too late.

'He's gone.'

Saki rested her cheek on her hand and smiled. *Oh the joy of being young.*

'Sorry about Reiji,' said Nanako, bowing her head to Nagare as an apology for Reiji abandoning his post like that.

'Oh, that's OK. No problem. Come to think of it, today . . .' Nagare smiled, and after glancing over at Reiko, exchanged looks with Saki. She looked at her watch.

'Yes, today,' she muttered.

Nanako looked over at the still-swinging door at the entrance.

'The only thing he's better at than anyone is his ability to never give up on a dream,' she said with a heavy sigh.

Observing Nanako looking over at the door, Saki thought, *But you like him, just as he is.* Biting her tongue so as not to voice her observation out loud, she smiled at Nanako.

'What is it?'

'Oh, nothing . . .' said Saki as she picked up *One Hundred Questions* from where Sachi had left it. She had no intention of continuing with the book; she just needed a distraction to stop herself from blurting out something stupid.

Then, just as an awkward pause began between Nanako and Saki . . .

'How much, please?' asked Reiko, standing up abruptly.

'What? Err . . . OK . . . Umm.'

Nagare appeared clearly agitated.

The cafe would close soon. It was quite natural for Reiko to think of leaving. Yet for some reason, Nagare was flustered and in a panic.

'How about a refill?' he suggested, together with a muddle of other suggestions.

'No, thanks. I'll pay now . . .' Reiko replied quietly, holding up the bill.

'Huh? But you've only just arrived,' he added, continuing with his string of odd comments. Reiko came to the cafe with Saki today about an hour earlier. She had finished the tea she ordered upon arriving and now he had no reason to stop her.

However, Reiko didn't simply seem to be pondering leaving. She was staring silently towards the door.

'Yukika is not coming, so . . .' she mumbled with a fading voice.

'Oh, but.'

Sweat beading from his brow, Nagare was clearly agitated at his own verbal inadequacies. Saki pitched in to rescue him.

'Were you waiting for Yukika?' She did not run counter to Reiko's words. Her voice was gentle and soothing.

'Yes,' replied Reiko as she stood there. 'She promised to introduce me to her boyfriend next time we met.'

'Oh, I bet you're looking forward to that.'

'But I think I must have got my days mixed up . . .'

Reiko's expression darkened.

It wasn't the days that were mixed up. Reiko's sister Yukika had died three months ago. Reiko had started to endlessly wait for her though she would never walk through the cafe door again.

It wasn't just today. It had been going on for a while. Every now and then, Reiko had been visiting the cafe and saying the same thing. Saki, of course, knew Yukika was dead. She had even tended to Yukika's mental care during her stay in hospital.

However, Saki was not going to pull Reiko up on that.

'Why don't you wait a little longer? She might have been late meeting her boyfriend.'

A faint glimmer appeared in Reiko's gloomy eyes.

'After all, you don't have to be anywhere, do you?'

'Er, no, I guess not.'

'There you go then . . .'

Reiko, once again, looked over at the door.'

'Let me buy you a coffee.' Saki looked at Nagare as she spoke.

'Ah, righto.' Nagare hastily withdrew to the kitchen.

'. . . OK. I'll stay a bit longer.'

Reiko slowly sat down again.

'How wonderful!'

Even while at work, Yukika's voice carried easily throughout the cafe.

'Shh. Your voice is too loud,' said Reiko, sitting at the counter. She was shrinking, fearful that other customers might stare at her. During the tourist season, Yukika would sometimes work at the cafe – it could be at full capacity throughout

the day, which was too much for Yukari and Reiji to handle
on their own. On occasion, Nanako would help out too.

The time of this particular conversation was in May, slap
bang in the middle of Golden Week, Japan's peak holiday season, and several weeks before Yukita was hospitalized. Cherry
blossom festivals were being held at Goryokaku and Hakodate parks and the cafe was constantly filled with customers.

It was just after the lunchtime peak, and it was becoming
a little less busy inside the cafe. There was still no time to be
taking a break, but there was enough leeway for Yukika to
enjoy a conversation with her older sister Reiko, who had
popped in as a customer.

'Finally, huh?'

Yukika had sat herself down alongside Reiko and was
looking into her face joyfully.

'Finally? What do you mean?'

'Put yourself in Mamoru's shoes.'

Having swivelled Reiko round by the stool to face her,
Yukika had leapt into full-on preaching mode.

'I don't know what you weren't satisfied with, but it's definitely not normal to make a guy wait six months to get an
answer to his proposal.'

'There were lots of things.'

'Lots of things? Like what?'

'. . . Lots of things are lots of things!'

Reiko and Yukika were the only members of their family.
Both parents had died when they were young, and they had
been taken in by relatives in Hakodate. Once Reiko started
working, the two sisters moved to an apartment and they got
on well living together. If Reiko got married, she would begin

that new life and leave her little sister behind. That was probably the *lots of things* she was referring to.

'I don't know why you don't tell me.'

'It's nothing you need to be concerned with. It hasn't been a trouble for you, has it?'

'Really?'

'Has it?'

'I've only been waiting on the sidelines . . . waiting for my sister to tie the knot first so I could go forward with my life.'

'Huh? Don't tell me you have a boyfriend?'

'Of course I have, what are you talking about?'

The news that Yukika had a boyfriend came right out of the blue for Reiko. She thought Yukika was still a child. Or, rather, she wanted to think of her as one.

'Why are you looking so surprised?' Yukika's tone was accusing, as if calling Reiko out for treating her as a child.

'Oh, I didn't know . . . Have you really? Will you get married?'

'Well, maybe, if he proposed,' she said lifting up her chin alluding to more.

'OK . . . So he's not proposed?'

'Not exactly proposed . . .'

'Wow . . .'

There was a little a sadness, but deep down, Reiko felt relieved. True, she had felt guilty at the thought of getting married and leaving her sister behind, but she also wanted happiness for Yukika. She had long wished that her sister would find a special partner. And Yukika had the same feeling, no doubt.

'Yeah, it's good! There's no rush, but I feel I could say yes if he asked.'

Yukika seemed careful to indicate she was not about to jump in and beat her to the aisle. But that wasn't acknowledged by Reiko.

'Aren't you going to let me meet him?' she asked.

This time, Reiko swivelled Yukika around by the stool to face her.

'No way.'

'What?'

'Absolutely, no.'

'Well you can't get married if you don't introduce him to me, can you?'

'Why not?'

'You know perfectly well why not. There might be just two of us, but we're still a family.'

'Yes, but that surely doesn't mean I have to get your approval!'

'Does so.'

'Does not.'

'Let me meet him.'

'No way.'

'Well, why not?'

'Where to start?'

They were enjoying the snappy back and forth.

'Is he too frivolous?'

'No.'

'Ah, so he's a 3B?'

'What's that?'

'Guys who are charming but make terrible boyfriends: bartender, beautician and band member.'

'No.'

'So, he's a 3F!'

'3F?'

'Fitness instructor, fireman, fisherman.'

'You're just listing jobs starting with F.'

'Tell me about him.'

'No.'

'He works in a theatre company?'

'Oh, get real.'

'A wannabe comedian?'

'Hell no.'

That touched a nerve with Reiji, just behind the two. 'I heard that!' he interjected.

'I want to meet him. Come on, introduce him to me!'

'OK, fine! I'll introduce him next time.'

'When?'

'I don't know when. Next time . . .'

'Really? Promise?'

'Yes, yes.'

'OK then.'

Reiko presented her little finger.

'What are you doing?' Yukika said with questioning eyebrows.

'Swearing on our pinkies, silly.'

'That's not necessary, is it?'

'Sure it is, come on.'

Yukika reluctantly presented her little finger and Reiko latched hers onto it.

'Keep the pinkie promise . . .'

'Reiko, your voice is too loud!'

'. . . or swallow a thousand needles!'

The day when they exchanged that promise – when Yukika was still alive – was a dreamlike happy moment.

Yukika was gone from her life.

She died leaving nothing behind but her promise. She only lasted a month after entering hospital. It was a fleeting moment; her departure was so sudden that it greatly disturbed Reiko. Reiko first suffered insomnia. Then, after days of continual sleepless nights, she began to feel like she was living in a dream, even during the day. Gradually, she was unable to even differentiate between dream and reality. Even while awake, the slightest thing would prompt her to see a dream of the day in the cafe when she made that promise with Yukika.

These were daytime hallucinations. The symptoms were serious enough to be considered a psychiatric disorder, and she had to receive counselling from Saki. With Reiko unable to go through with her marriage to Mamoru, which had made Yukika so happy, the plans were put on hold.

Reiko couldn't bear the thought of being happy when her beloved younger sister had died. If her insomnia continued like this, her condition was bound to deteriorate. It would debilitate her, to the point that it would cloud her consciousness, making it impossible to make the correct judgements. Saki was worried that left unchecked, Reiko might be overwhelmed by the compulsive idea that she too must be unhappy like her sister, putting her at risk of suicide.

Yukika had occupied a large part of Reiko's life.

There was nothing anyone could say to rescue Reiko from her current state of mind.

A bright flash.

'Ah,' gasped Nanako in response.

The entire room had lit up brightly for a moment, and then after a few seconds, a thunderous rumbling rang out.

'It's pretty close,' remarked Nagare.

Outside the window, heavy rain started pelting down loudly.

'I hope Reiji is OK.'

When he left the cafe, he wasn't carrying an umbrella. Even if he found a place to shelter from the rain, he would probably get soaked if he came back without an umbrella on his way home. At the end of October, the rain was cold.

'I can't let him catch a cold,' said Nanako standing up from the counter stool. 'Could I borrow an umbrella?' She pointed to the umbrella stand.

'Yeah, sure,' replied Nagare. 'Be careful out there.'

It was dark outside; the lightning was getting closer, and getting struck by it wasn't entirely impossible.

'OK.' Nanako let out an annoyed sigh, but she was moving quickly. It was as if she had been searching for a reason to chase after Reiji. She grabbed two umbrellas from the stand and then left the cafe in haste.

DA-DING-DONG

After Nanako left, silence pervaded the cafe. Only the rain pattering against the window and the ticking of the clock could be heard.

Nagare and Saki were staring at the clock. It was six forty-five.

'I think you'll definitely meet Yukika today . . .'

Then, just as Saki muttered this to Reiko, there was another bright flash of light from the window.

PEWN

Suddenly the lights in the cafe went out.

'Ah . . .'

It was a power cut.

After a slight delay, the crash and boom of the thunder hit.

It would take anywhere between a few minutes or a few hours until power was restored. The fact that it was caused by a lightning strike made it even more unpredictable.

'Must be a blackout.'

'It's so dark.'

Nagare and Saki exchanged words calmly. It was as if they expected the power to go out.

The darkness was so sudden everyone's eyes had not yet adapted, and they were completely invisible to each other. However, a sound of clothes rustling and shoes clicking could be heard that belonged to someone other than themselves. Without anyone noticing, someone else had entered – or, strictly speaking, appeared.

It wasn't Nanako. This new presence was felt from the chair of the black-suited old gentleman, and that gentleman had no such presence. As a ghost, he never rustled his clothes or clicked his shoes, even while on his trip to the toilet.

This clear presence meant only one thing – someone had travelled from the past or the future.

'. . . Reiko?'

'Huh?'

Reiko turned confusedly to the direction from where the voice had come.

At that moment, the cafe lights suddenly turned back on.

'The power's back,' muttered Nagare in a soft voice.

'Reiko.'

Reiko's eyes were fixed on the owner of that voice. 'Yukika?'

Sitting in that chair was Reiko's deceased younger sister, Yukika. In contrast with Reiko's lily-white complexion, Yukika's expression was bright, and her posture, straight. Her eyes, gazing directly at Reiko, were lively.

'Is that really you?' asked Reiko as she slowly rose from her chair. Her voice was wavering.

'Yes, it's me.'

In comparison, Yukika's voice sounded bubbly. There was a stark contrast in tone between the two. Her sister, appearing before her, was behaving just like her sister in her daydreams: winsome and carefree.

'Did you wait? Sorry, I'm a bit late . . .'

She poked out her tongue and smiled foolishly. Her expression was just as it had been on that day.

'Reiko?'

'Yukika, is that really you?'

'What's wrong? You look like a deer caught in the headlights.'

Yukika tilted her head inquisitively and studied Reiko's face.

Is this a dream? Reiko was muddled and lost for words.

'Reiko?'

Yukika's tone sounded concerned. Reiko was in a panic.

'Oh, do I?' Reiko said. She managed a smile, but it seemed a little out of practice.

But Yukika wasn't interested in making a thing of Reiko's disorientation.

'Wow! Outside looks amazing. The autumn leaves are so pretty!'

She stared out of the window excitedly and took in the autumn leaves, which looked like dancing flames under the lights.

'Doesn't it look beautiful?'

'Yes, I suppose,' Reiko replied with a struggle. She was caught in dismay, trying to work out in her head how her sister had suddenly appeared.

'You seem distracted,' Yukika said, pouting.

'No, no I'm not,' said Reiko, still disoriented but attempting to gain her composure. She walked over to Yukika until she was close enough to reach out and touch her.

'. . . Reiko?' Yukika said, studying her sister's face.

'What?'

'You look pale. Are you OK?'

'Do I?'

'Uh-huh.'

'It's probably just the dim lighting.'

'Oh, OK.'

She was the same. Her little sister, unchanged from that day, was here, good-natured, charming and friendly.

Her kind, forever smiley sister, always worrying about others, was here. After staring at her for a while, Reiko finally worked it out. *She's come from the past.*

But Reiko was clueless about the reason for her sister's visit. She couldn't read anything from her expression. Yukika picked up the cup of coffee before her and took a sip.

'Eeww . . .' She scrunched her face and poked out her tongue from the bitterness. Yukika's simple gesture of wincing at bitter coffee was enough to tear at Reiko's heart. Her sister was meant to be dead and yet, here she was, before her eyes. She had never imagined that she would see her sister again.

Yukika turned to Nagare. 'Excuse me,' she said, raising her hand. 'Can I have some milk?'

'Oh, sorry, I'll get you some.' he went into the kitchen.

A thought came to Reiko. *Yukika is meant to be dead . . .*

With her mind clouded by lack of sleep and fatigue, Reiko had been stuck in her dream world; but that thought instantly pulled her back to reality.

She died . . .

Reiko did not want to believe it or acknowledge it. Like some desperate people drowning their sorrows in alcohol, she was attempting to escape the pain of reality by not sleeping. Tormenting herself was a way to keep a lid on the heartache of losing her sister.

But the Yukika appearing before her was neither a dream nor an illusion. That much Reiko clearly understood. How could she possibly mistake her sister in all her realness?

Emerging from the rock-bottom turbid depths of despair of losing her sister, her mind was gradually finding clarity.

She might not . . .

A thought crossed Reiko's mind. Yukika appeared exactly the same as when she was alive. That probably meant Yukika was here, completely unaware that she was going to die.

It was plausible. No one knows what the future holds. Assuming the Yukika here now had come from a time before she was hospitalized, then how could she even know she would get ill and die?

'Here you go.'

Nagare had returned holding a milk pot.

'Wow . . .'

Yukika's wide round eyes were not focused on the milk pot but looking up at Nagare standing before her. Yukika, who died before Nagare came to Hakodate, was meeting him for the first time, and she did not conceal her surprise as she looked up at his two-metre stature.

'Oh, thank you.'

Curiosity sparkled from her eyes as she nodded courteously. She had never met anyone so tall before.

Reiko felt doubly sure as she observed Yukika's as-always carefree spontaneity: *She doesn't know she will die.* After all, how could one behave so brightly while knowing of one's death? *But if not that, why would she come from the past . . . ?*

Doubt was swirling unresolved in Reiko's mind. She didn't know. She felt sure of one thing alone: *I can't let Yukika realize that she has died.*

The click of a switch sounded inside her head.

She realized: *Just like Yukika, I too must act like the big sister I always was.* And almost instantly a liveliness returned to Reiko's eyes.

'Yukika.'

'Hm? What is it?' she replied while stirring in the milk and sugar she had added to the coffee.

'How's your boyfriend?'

What better place to start a natural conversation than continuing on from that other day . . .

'Huh? Oh, err . . .' Yukika's eyes darted this way and that as she hung on the last syllable.

I know that response.

Yukika was behaving as she always did when wanting to sidestep the topic.

'You don't mean to tell me that you've split up, do you?'

'How do you know?'

'I could tell just by looking at you!'

Is this why? Did she come from the past to tell me this? Why would that be even necessary?

Unaware of Reiko's thought processes, Yukika shrugged her shoulders and said playfully, 'Oh Reiko, you're so you!'

'Oh what? I was looking forward to meeting him.'

Then why did she come?

'Oh, it doesn't matter, he was no big deal.'

'Breaking up so easily, it's not right.'

'I didn't say it was easy.' Yukika puffed out her cheeks.

Reiko still didn't know what Yukika had come to do.

But . . .

I never could have imagined that this, this casual conversation could make me so happy.

Then she realized. Yukika would feel the same. *If she knew I had broken up with Mamoru, she would be upset too. Just as I had wished for her happiness, she was the most elated about my engagement with Mamoru.*

'Well, I don't know the story . . .' Reiko also puffed out her cheeks. On countless occasions since they were little, this sisterly back and forth had played out.

But that was no more.

I'm sorry. Mamoru and I . . .

Reiko gently closed her eyes to stop herself from crying.

Yukika had to return to the past before the coffee got cold. Even Reiko knew that cafe rule. *Well, given the circumstances, I want to play big sister until we part ways for ever. I don't want to give her anything to worry over. I don't care if that means lying . . .*

Clenching her fists tightly, Reiko took a deep breath as though she was resolving not to say anything that would cause Yukika to catch on to their reality. She breathed out slowly.

'Well unlike you, Mamoru and I are going well . . .' she reported, careful not to let her voice quaver.

It's going to be fine. I sounded convincing . . .

'Really?'

I can't let her find out.

'Yes, of course. We are holding the ceremony next month. Why, you . . .'

She mustn't realize.

'. . . you'll be there of course.'

I can't cry.

But her vision was wavering.

Why did you die, why?

'I mean, if you don't come to my wedding, I'll never forgive you, right?'

As she said this, Reiko had intended to look at Yukika with a full smile . . .

'Uh-huh.'

. . . but a single trickle of tears was running down Yukika's face.

PEWN

Just then, the cafe again fell into darkness. No one could see.

'Oh, not again!' Nagare grumbled.

When a blackout was caused by lightning striking a power pole, the power would go on and off repeatedly to pinpoint the pole.

'. . . Yukika?'

Was she crying?

'Oh . . . it's no good. Reiko, your lying is atrocious.'

Only Yukika's almost pettish voice resounded in the darkness.

'Oh no, I knew this would happen.'

'What are you talking about?'

'Reiko, you've split up with Mamoru, haven't you?'

What?

'No. We haven't split up. Why would you think that?'

'Don't lie.'

'I'm telling you the truth!'

'Then why are you crying?'

'What? I'm not crying.'

'You're crying.'

'What are you talking about? You can't even see my face; it's so dark.'

'I can see.'

'Huh?'

'I know Reiko, without having to see your face. I know your heart . . .'

'Yukika . . .'

'Reiko, I'm so sorry . . . It's my fault for dying.'

What is she saying?

'Yukika . . . ?'

It was just voices; nothing could be seen in the dark.

'Ah-huh-huh . . .'

The sound of Yukika's sobbing mixed in with the ticking of the pendulum clock could be heard amid the silence.

'I was determined not to cry . . . but it's no good . . .'

'Yukika . . .'

'I've been told I'm really ill . . . and I've only got a month to live . . . I still feel completely fine. Unbelievable right? But that's what they told me . . .'

Now nothing made sense. Reiko's emotions were running amok. Totally unable to think, she was only able to grasp one fact.

My little sister knows she is going to die.

'Why though? Why do you have to die?'

'I know, right? I feel the same.'

'Yukika . . .'

'But what's really strange is the thought of dying is not so scary . . .'

That can't be true! Why are you crying then!

She couldn't say it, though. In place of words, a flurry of tears poured from her eyes.

'What scares me . . .'

Yukika paused to take a big sniff.

'Is just that I'm worried that you will forget how to smile when I die . . .'

'Even with surgery, we can't help you . . .'

It was early summer when her doctor explained the illness to her. The evening was unusually hot and humid for Hakodate.

'It's not that we've never seen it before, it's just that the disease is so rare we can only offer you our best efforts . . .'

'I see.'

'We can explain to your family . . .'

'No, please don't say anything.'

'But . . .'

'When it's necessary, I'll tell them directly. But right now . . .'

'Understood.'

Yukika had the doctors tell Reiko that they found a shadow on her lung X-ray and she was going into hospital for tests as soon as a bed became available. 'It will be fine. There's nothing to worry about,' Yukika said with a smile. But Reiko's reaction was unexpectedly excessive. She persistently wanted to know everything good and bad about her physical condition, and whenever Yukika looked even the slightest bit tired, Reiko's complexion would turn off-colour, making her the one who looked unwell. It was Saki who noticed the abnormality.

'Generalized anxiety disorder?' Yukika said to Saki, knitting her brow at the unfamiliar medical term.

Saki was a cafe regular. She ate there every morning and dropped in for a coffee after work, so she was well acquainted with Yukika and had been for some time. That naturally meant she knew Reiko as well. When Saki had noticed Reiko's behaviour, she reached out to Yukika.

'Reiko has always been a worrier. Is now any different from that?'

'It's not something you can clearly delineate, but normally you draw the line based on whether the anxiety could require treatment.'

'You think she requires treatment?'

'Anyone can get anxious, like when you can't remember locking up before going out, right?'

'Right.'

'But someone with this condition can feel enormous anxiety about daily life issues, which can lead to side effects like not being able to sleep or eat. It can be a real problem.'

Yukika's heart skipped a beat.

'There are many causes and triggers, but in Reiko's case, I think it might stem from your parents dying in an accident.'

'Why do you think that?'

'I get the sense that Reiko is hounded by the anxiety of death. Like she is struggling with not knowing when or understanding why people die. On top of that, with her strong sense of responsibility, Reiko has a strong sense of mission as the elder sister to raise you as a mother and father would.'

Everything that Saki was saying was hitting the mark.

'About you going into hospital, it's just for tests, right? If Reiko is getting physical and mental problems from overly worrying that you might die and what she can do about it, I think she requires treatment.'

Yukika hadn't yet told Saki about her illness. However, it didn't seem right to stay quiet now. Especially since Saki was able to describe Reiko's situation so accurately.

'. . . Dr Muraoka, I haven't been completely forthcoming.'

Yukika then opened up about everything – that if the surgery was unsuccessful, she would only have about one month to live.

'But Reiko . . .'

'I don't want her to know.'

'I understand how you feel, but.'

'I might not die . . . If I told Reiko that I could die, well she . . .'

Just imagining Reiko's sorrow and pain was enough to grip Yukika's heart tightly. No one wants to see the most important person in their life suffer because of their own actions. And telling her those words, *I could die*, would tear both her own heart and Reiko's to shreds.

'I'd be lying if I said I wasn't afraid of dying. What scares me more, though, is the thought that Reiko might stop smiling if I die . . .'

'Oh, Yukika darling.'

'Reiko has finally decided to get married to Mamoru, and just as she has her happiness in front of her, I could be about to ruin it . . .'

'So, please smile . . .'

Yukika's voice sounded far from pitiful as it echoed in the pitch blackness of the power outage. She was keeping it cheerful for as long as she stayed alive, wishing only for her sister's happiness. Reiko couldn't ignore that voice, and the feeling behind it.

'Don't tell me you came from the past to tell me that?'

'Yes. That's all I wanted to say. Nothing else.'

'Yukika . . .'

'Even if I am dead, I want you to live with a smile on your face! Then I'll always be watching your happy smile.'

She had been holding back her tears with all her might, but a slight sniffling could be heard.

'In the half a month I've got left, I'll also live with a smile.'

'Yukika.'

'Well?'

'Yukika.'

'Will you do that for me?'

'Yukika.'

'How about an answer?'

'Um . . .'

'Huh?'

'Fine. Yes.'

'Great!'

Just from hearing Yukika's voice, even in the total darkness, Reiko could clearly picture her good-natured, charming, friendly, kind, always-worrying-about-others smile.

'Yukika . . .'

It was then that Reiko realized . . .

I've been mistaken.

If the tables had been reversed . . .

I would not have been afraid of dying, but I definitely would not want Yukika to suffer over my death.

Reiko realized that Yukika was feeling exactly the same way.

I can't change the fact of Yukika's death . . .

But I can live in a way that won't cause Yukika sorrow!

A large tear fell from Reiko's eye.

Sisters with the same sentiment.

Then Reiko understood.

What if the tables were turned?

If I had died, and Yukika was mourning my death, the one in deepest despair . . . would be me.

I shouldn't have broken off my engagement with Mamoru, which had made Yukika so happy . . .

For Yukika's sake, I mustn't be unhappy . . .

Reiko closed her eyes tightly as if she were biting down hard on her feelings towards Yukika.

But that didn't stop the overflowing tears.

Reiko desperately tried to wipe away her tears.

I can't let Yukika see my face like this. I should be living with a smile as Yukika wishes. I can't be crying. I'll need to be smiling as if everything is fine if the lights come on now!

At that moment,

CLINK . . .

The sound of a coffee cup being placed on a saucer came from the darkness where Yukika was sitting.

Reiko knew instantly what that meant: Yukika must have finished her coffee.

Is it over already?

'Yukika!'

My little sister . . .

'Reiko.'

My winsome, adorable and kind sister . . .

'Yukika . . .'

'I love you, Reiko. I love you.'

I'm sorry you've had to worry about me . . .

'You must, absolutely must . . .'

My forever-smiling little sister . . .

'. . . become happy, OK?'

Yukika . . .

'Can you promise me?'

'Yes, I promise,' Reiko replied, smiling her hardest.

Nothing could be seen in the complete darkness. Her flowing tears had by no means stopped. But still, Reiko was giving her fullest smile in Yukika's direction.

I'll be fine.

With that thought framing her mind, Reiko was certain that just as she sensed in her heart Yukika's smile, Yukika too must be sensing her smile, even if it was completely dark.

'. . . Good.' That was Yukika's final softly voiced reply. It no longer felt like anyone was there. A silent stillness had returned. Only the rain falling outside the window and the ticking of the clock could be heard.

'. . . Yukika?'

There was no reply to Reiko's call.

BIP

Shortly after that, the lights came back on. Yukika was no longer sitting in the chair. In her place sat the gentleman in the black suit. He was still and settled as if he had been there all along.

'This postcard arrived from Yukari,' muttered Nagare from behind Reiko. He passed it to her once she turned around. It said the following.

On 28th October at 6.47 p.m., a young woman by
the name of Yukika Nunokawa will appear. Make
sure that her sister Reiko is there waiting. Ask
Dr Muraoka for details.
Yukari. (28th July)

Based on the date, Yukari must have written it directly after arriving in America. The postmark said, 'WEST HART-FORD CT'. Located in central Hartford County, Connecticut, the town of West Hartford has its fair share of upscale residential areas. Yukari must have sent the card from a port of call on her journey to find the missing father of the boy who had visited the cafe.

Reiko's gaze shifted from the postcard to Saki, demanding an explanation. Saki sighed. 'To be honest, I was startled when she announced she was going to the future.'

'I'll leave it to your judgement, Dr Muraoka. If Reiko has broken up with Mamoru three months after I die, please bring her here.'

It was after closing at the cafe, and Yukika had her head bowed down low. Saki was certainly uncomfortable with the sudden request. But with Yukika's expression so unwavering, all she could do was nod. Yukari, who was watching from the side, seemed convinced, based on that expression alone, that Yukika was going to the future.

But Saki did have some niggling concerns.

'I don't mean to step in your way, but how can you be sure you'll meet?'

Saki was familiar with its rules. For Yukika's plan to work, just getting herself to the future was not enough; she also had to make sure Reiko was there, otherwise they would not meet. Another unknown was that Saki could not foresee how Reiko would fare mentally after Yukika's death. She wasn't blind to the worst-case scenario of Reiko following after Yukika by committing suicide. It came with her job to consider all possibilities.

'If you ask me, I think you should be honest with Reiko

about your illness. I also think it would be better for Reiko if she was made aware of her own problems . . .'

That was Saki's rational opinion as a psychiatrist.

If Yukika never knew this cafe existed, she wouldn't even have the choice to go to the future. Moreover, Saki did believe that if Yukika talked it through with Reiko, then Reiko's mental state would not deteriorate as badly as Yukika feared it would. Saki also knew of many people who had got over the unfortunate death of a loved one. So rather than gambling on things turning out in the future, it would be more sensible to change Reiko's present reality. That's what she meant. But perhaps it was not that Yukika didn't understand. Without any change in facial expression, she nodded.

'I know I should,' she said.

Then she laid out her counter.

'It's selfish of me, I know. If I was putting Reiko's interests first, I'm sure it would be best to do as you say . . . But if I tell Reiko I'm ill and will probably die soon, I will have to spend my last days watching her in despair. I don't want that. I want to have as many days as possible with Reiko smiling. I don't want to tell her about my illness. I just don't and I can't bear the thought of Reiko becoming unhappy because of my death. So, if Reiko has broken up with Mamoru, then I want you to bring her to meet me in the future. I'll do something about it. I'll try to fix things somehow.'

Saki was left speechless by Yukika's wishes.

'Why not just let her go?' chimed in Yukari. 'Yukika already knows what will happen, right? Sisters know each other like that. She knows how her death could affect Reiko.

Yukika, I think you are the only one who knows the best thing to do, right? Don't you think?'

'Yes.'

Yukika nodded avidly.

'All right, I'll do it. But I take no responsibility for what happens,' Saki said in a resigned tone.

Yukika knew that even if her trip to the future didn't affect Reiko as she hoped, she could count on Saki to do her best in providing treatment for Reiko. That went without saying.

It was therefore settled. 'Thank you so much!' she said, bowing gratefully.

'Right then, are you ready?'

Yukari was already holding the silver kettle.

'Yes.'

'Before the coffee gets cold . . .'

'I was not in a position to refuse,' Saki apologized. 'No matter how much suffering you had to endure . . .' she said, her eyes filling with tears.

Making that choice had obviously been difficult for Saki as well. Had she not been a psychiatrist, she might not have found it so tough. It had been with self-reproach that she had weighed up Yukika's wishes against Reiko's condition. As a result, she was in tears, apologizing for putting Yukika's wishes ahead of Reiko's, despite Reiko's potential suffering. She deserved whatever blame Reiko cast on her.

But Reiko looked at Saki. 'I think it was for the best,' she said kindly. 'I got to see my darling little sister's smiling face one more time . . .'

Despite the large tears spilling out of them, her eyes were full of life. Gone was the empty and unfocused look she had worn for the past few months. Now they were full of hope, with a firm resolve on how she should live from now on.

It had stopped raining a little earlier. Outside the window, stars appeared in the night sky.

Reiko bowed politely to Saki and Nagare and left the cafe.

DA-DING-DONG

The bell rang out softly.

'Will she be OK?' wondered Nagare, as he watched Reiko's figure fade out into the night.

'Well, she probably won't suddenly be fine,' Saki said and looked out of the window. 'The present hasn't changed. Yukika is still dead. I can't imagine her sadness and loneliness will just disappear.'

Nagare drew a long sigh. 'No,' he muttered.

Saki had pointed out the exact thing he was concerned about. But Saki had not meant to say it in a pessimistic way.

'But in the end, the promise Reiko made to Yukika has brought her a light of hope, which has lit up what had gone completely dark. It won't change what happened to Yukika, but I do hope it will make a big difference to Reiko's future.'

The light that Yukika brought was guiding Reiko to happiness and it was also a guiding light for Yukika's happiness. After all, Reiko's happiness itself was happiness for Yukika.

'For sure, that would be good.' Nagare nodded. He remembered his own wife, Kei.

Kei was born with a weak body. When she was pregnant with Miki, the doctor told her that her body would not be able to endure giving birth. Having a baby was certain to mean early death. Although he never said it out loud, aborting the baby was a thought that had crossed his mind.

Kei was resolutely determined to have the baby, and she was not afraid to die. But as a woman, she could only give birth. She wouldn't be there for her child after she was born. She wouldn't be there by her child's side during times of sadness or loneliness. She wouldn't be there to listen to worries, or to lend a hand. She wanted her child to be happy, but no matter how much she wished for her child's happiness, her anxiety would grow, and frighteningly so. Her body was reaching her limit and if she crossed that threshold, her child's life would also be in peril.

On the day when there was nothing that she could do but go to hospital to focus purely on safely delivering the baby, she found herself staring at *the* chair, which was empty. It was as if it were calling her, responding to her heart's cries . . .

Ever since the cafe opened, the chair was known as the 'seat that sent you to the past'. But it could also send you to the future. It was simply the case that no customer had ever really wanted to go to the future. That was because even if you decided to go to a certain day in the future, no one could know whether the person you wanted to meet would be there. The time that coffee takes to get cold is fleeting. Even if you got someone to promise to be there on the day, any number of things could occur to waylay them. That made the chances of meeting quite slim.

The period of time Yukika travelled to meet Reiko was around four months. It was not that difficult to arrange their meeting thanks to the cooperation of her friends at the cafe, who made sure Reiko didn't leave.

In contrast, Kei had to travel ten years into the future to meet Miki, but she made a mistake and actually travelled fifteen years. Such errors were more likely to occur and this made meeting someone in the future that much more unpredictable.

Even so, there were ways to ensure they happened. In Kei's case, it was through a phone conversation with Nagare that she realized her mistake – that she had arrived fifteen years into the future and that the girl in front of her was her daughter. In this way, Kei was successfully able to meet Miki.

Kei had been blaming herself for not being around for her daughter's life. When Miki told her, 'I'm really glad for the life you gave me,' Kei felt a wash of relief. Miki's words had been a tremendous emotional support for Kei. If she had continued to grapple with that anxiety, Kei might not have lived long enough to give birth to Miki.

'Thank you for having me,' Miki had told her mother, and these words of hers gave Kei an energy that we call hope.

Inside every person is an inherent capability to make it through any kind of difficulty. Everyone has that energy. But sometimes when that energy flows via our anxiety valve, the flow can be restricted. The greater the anxiety, the greater the strength needed to open the valve and release the energy.

That strength is empowered by hope. You could say that hope is the power to believe in the future.

Miki's words gave Kei that power. Her body gave out after giving birth, but Kei never lost her smile.

Likewise, Reiko was given the hope to live from Yukika. That hope came from the realization that the best way to make Yukika happy was for Reiko to work towards her own happiness.

Reiji and Nanako were returning to the cafe together. He had left his shift early to perform a guerrilla live street comedy performance, and Nanako had chased after him to give him an umbrella. Reiji planned to help Nagare close the cafe, even if most of the work would already be finished, and Nanako had left her bag behind.

'So pretty,' Nanako remarked about the star-filled sky. The visibility was excellent because of the rain earlier that evening. A night like this one was the best time to view the nightscape from the top of Mount Hakodate.

There are several stories that are told about that night-scape. One tells of a jinx that 'if you propose while looking at the nightscape from Mount Hakodate, you will split up'. Such jinx stories are told across Japan. In Tokyo, couples who ride in a boat on the pond of the renowned Inokashira Park will not last long together; in Miyagi Prefecture, lovers who cross the Fukuura Bridge in Matsushima will break up. Other places with the jinx related to couples splitting up include the Tsurugaoka Hachimangu Shinto shrine in Kamakura, Kanagawa Prefecture due to the tale of Lady Shizuka Gozen developing a grudge from getting torn from her lover, the military commander Yoshitsune, by the shogun Minamoto no Yoritomo according to one theory and the jealousy of the shogun's wife Hojo Masako according to another. Mount Hakodate falls into that category of places, perhaps reflecting its image as a sightseeing spot for tourists.

Another story is that when you view a nightscape from Mount Hakodate, you can find hidden hearts. There are several versions of this story, including 'if you find three hearts, you will find happiness', and 'your wish will come true'. Though of course, no evidence has come to light to support any of those stories.

As locals, Reiji and Nanako probably knew of the jinx of Mount Hakodate, but Reiji had no interest in nightscapes or night skies. Rather than walking alongside Nanako, Reiji was walking ahead of her.

The cafe was located on the mountainside and the walk back commanded a beautiful view of the city's lights. It could be quite the romantic walk for a couple.

However, their conversation was anything but. The two were discussing whether Reiji had really memorized all of *One Hundred Questions*.

'OK, what was question thirty-five?'

'Whether you would return something borrowed.'

'What about question fifty-one, then?'

'Whether you would cash in the ten-million-yen lottery ticket you won.'

'Question fifty-five?'

'Whether you would go ahead and hold the wedding ceremony.'

'You really memorized them all?'

'Oh, it's not that big a deal.'

'It's amazing!'

'It's just like learning material for a comedy skit.'

'Why don't you get serious at university?' Nanako asked.

She meant that he could be getting good grades. As a close friend since childhood, Nanako knew that Reiji had always achieved excellent grades in middle and high school. She was also implying that he could aspire to be a comedian after he finished university.

'It seems pointless.'

'Why?'

'As soon as I pass my audition, I want to go to Tokyo, like, immediately. So right now, I want to work as much as I can to save some money.'

Hearing Reiji's answer, Nanako ever so slightly slowed her gait.

They were approaching the cafe.

'Reiji,' Nanako called out, stopping completely. The night breeze felt nice on her cheeks.

'. . . Huh?' Reiji turned around. Nanako's new lipstick glowed amidst the lights of the town and the fiery autumn leaves.

Reiji felt some kind of stirring in his chest again.

'Look . . .'

Nanako was about to say something when . . .

Ching . . .

Reiji's phone chimed. It was the notification sound for a new mail. But Reiji didn't check his phone. He was more interested in what Nanako was about to say. His heart was astir.

'What?' he asked.

'Oh, nothing,' she replied, motioning that he should check his phone. She thought it could wait.

The exchange was the same as always. Apart from the stirring in Reiji's heart . . .

Reiji pulled the phone from his pocket and checked his inbox. Nanako looked down at the city lights of Hakodate while Reiji read his mail.

Here and there, light-ups of autumn leaves were being switched off.

Nanako noticed just then that a bell cricket was quietly chirping. Its barely audible cry sounded so lonely.

Do bell crickets really sound like that?

While Nanako was immersed in such thoughts, Reiji suddenly exclaimed, 'I don't believe it!'

Nanako's heart stirred, but it felt like foreboding.

'Why? What happened?' Riveted to the spot, she just called out to Reiji, peering at him from a few metres away.

'I got it.' His voice was distant.

'Got what?'

'The position I was auditioning for in Tokyo the other day . . .'

Reiji's eyes were wide in disbelief. 'I did it!' he said and jumped up high on the spot. He turned to Nanako, saying something too quickly to be intelligible, and galloped off to the cafe.

Nanako didn't remember anything after that.

All she could remember was the chirping of the bell cricket and how she forgot to say, 'Congratulations.'

IV

The Young Man

Hakodate received its first snowfall of the year on 13 November, which was about ten days later than usual. The colloquial term for wind-blown snow on a cloudless day is *wind flowers*. True to that description, the snowflakes fall like flower petals dancing in the wind. The window of the cafe offered a vivid and beautiful view of blue sky, and white snow on red autumn leaves.

DA-DING-DONG

The doorbell rang and Reiko entered the cafe.

Until last month, Reiko had had a hard time accepting her sister's death. She had been unable to sleep and was mentally unstable. Her condition improved, however, when she made a promise to her sister from the past that she would live a happy life. She appeared now with colour in her cheeks, dragging a suitcase with rattling wheels.

'Hello, welcome.'

It was Sachi who welcomed her. She was sitting at the counter alone.

Reiko looked around and cocked her head, puzzled. It wasn't uncommon for the cafe to be empty after lunch on a weekday, but not only were there no customers, but Kazu, who she expected to be behind the counter, was nowhere to be seen – nor was Nagare or even Reiji.

'Are you here alone, Sachi?'

Dragging her clattering suitcase, Reiko walked over to where she was sitting.

'Ah, yes,' Sachi replied while her eyes darted back and forth.

'Your mum?' She was referring to Kazu.

'Out shopping.'

'What about Nagare?'

'Uncle's downstairs on the phone.' Sachi pointed her finger to emphasize the point.

'OK, where's Reiji, then?'

'Tokyo.'

'Tokyo?'

'He passed his audition.'

Reiko had heard from her late sister that Reiji was an aspiring comedian. She had inadvertently seen him perform his gags several times, but never once did she find them funny. When she mentioned that to Yukika, Yukika said that 'the lack of funniness is the humour', but Reiko just didn't get it. Each time he tested one of his jokes, she endured his performance with a polite smile.

Given what she thought of his jokes, the news of him passing a Tokyo audition left her with mixed feelings.

'He did? Oh . . .'

Reiko thought it wise to ask no further about Reiji as she sat down next to Sachi. She would not know what to say if asked whether she thought Reiji's gags were funny or not. Children didn't give a second thought to asking tricky questions. Reiji may not have been there now, but had Reiko replied to such a question with a nuanced response, she imagined it could be relayed back to Reiji with a different interpretation. It was a scenario best avoided.

'How far have you got?'

'I've done them all.'

'Every one of them? That's impressive.'

'Yes.'

Partly due to the sleep deprivation she had suffered, Reiko's memories of the events leading up to her meeting with Yukika were vague blurs. Still, she could remember Sachi had been having fun with this book together with Dr Saki and Nanako.

'Was it fun?'

'It was fun!'

'I wish I had had a turn.'

Reiko meant it. She had been too preoccupied to show any interest in such things before.

'You want to do it now?'

Sachi's voice became loud and enthusiastic. She didn't know that until just a little while ago Reiko had been suffering from generalized anxiety disorder and was struggling to accept her sister's death. To her, Reiko was just another regular customer.

'Maybe I'll do just one question?' Reiko replied, looking at her watch. She had a flight to catch but there was at least enough time to make a small memory.

'Which question shall we do?'

'I'll let you choose.'

'All right then.'

Sachi flipped through the pages happily until she landed at one page.

'Let's do this one.'

'OK.'

'Ready?'

'Yes, go ahead.'

Sachi began reading aloud.

' "There is a man or woman with whom you are very much in love.

' "If the world were to end tomorrow, which would you do?

' "1. You propose to them.

' "2. You don't propose because there is no point." '

Sachi had asked the same question to Nanako and others, but this was the first time for Reiko.

'So, which would you do?' Sachi looked at Reiko, her eyes glistening in anticipation.

Reiko wasn't hiding her hesitation. If Yukika hadn't visited her from the past, she would have chosen 'two'. However, she was a different Reiko now.

'I think I'd choose "one",' she said, realizing as she spoke that she had a clear reason for choosing so.

'Why?'

Reiko pretended to think for a moment before happily replying, 'My sister would be furious if I turned down even one day of happiness.' No doubt she was picturing Yukika, who now resided in Reiko's head, nodding imperiously with her arms folded.

'Oh, I see,' Sachi also was nodding, seemingly satisfied.

A scuffling of footsteps could be heard coming up the stairs. Nagare had returned.

'Oh, hello, Reiko.'

'Hello.'

'What's up?' Nagare asked as he walked around the back of Reiko and Sachi and moved in behind the counter.

'I thought if I dropped by, I might get to say hello to Dr Saki.'

'Dr Saki?'

'Yes.'

'Oh? You didn't meet her just now? She was here a few moments ago . . .'

Nagare cocked his head as he looked at the chair Reiko was sitting in.

'Sachi, where'd Dr Saki go?'

'I don't know,' Sachi replied, for some reason oddly covering her face with the book.

'That's strange.'

On the counter was Sachi's orange juice and a half-finished coffee. There was no doubt that Saki had been there just earlier. Sachi was hiding something.

'Sachi . . .'

Nagare strengthened his tone as if trying to draw it out of her but she just hunched her shoulders.

'Oh, no, don't worry.'

'But . . .'

'Really, it's OK,' said Reiko, defending Sachi with a smile.

It was likely that Reiko had also noticed the coffee. Even if Sachi knew something, there was no reason to squeeze it out of her.

While casting a glance at Nagare as he softly sighed, Reiko spun her body round on her stool to face the chair on which the old gentleman sat. The memory of that day when she once again met Yukika flooded back.

'I still can't really believe it,' she muttered as if to herself. 'To think that she came to meet me . . .'

It was an understandable sentiment. Even though she knew the rules of this cafe, never in her wildest dreams had she expected her now deceased sister would come to see her. Even Nagare the cafe manager would be dismayed if Kei, his deceased wife, appeared before him.

'But thanks to her, I've decided to leave this place,' she said looking down at her suitcase. After her meeting with Yukika, Reiko had reconciled with Mamoru, if that was even the right word for it. It was only she who ever thought the relationship was over. On advice from Saki, Mamoru had simply taken a step back.

'Congratulations,' Nagare said bowing his head. He had learned from Saki that after the two had got back together, they had tied the knot at the register office.

DA-DING-DONG

Kazu had returned. With two grocery bags hanging from her hands, she looked like she was returning from shopping, just as Sachi had said.

'Hi, Mum!' Sachi ran over to her.

'Hi. Give me a hand please, dear,' Kazu said holding out one of the grocery bags. As Sachi took the bag, Kazu motioned with her eyes for her to take it downstairs. It contained their own private groceries.

'OK,' Sachi said energetically as she hurried off.

Nagare snorted, thinking, *She slipped out of that one well.*

Kazu noticed Reiko's suitcase.

'Oh, you're leaving today,' she remarked. She knew that Reiko and Mamoru had decided that their marriage was an opportune time to leave Hakodate.

'Yes.'

'Where was it that you're going to again?'

'Tokushima.'

Kazu passed the bag of groceries for the cafe over the counter to Nagare.

'Tokushima is renowned for its udon noodles, right?' asked Nagare, joining the discourse.

'Yes.'

'I've heard it's a nice place.'

'It's my husband's hometown.'

Nagare's eyes narrowed as he observed how Reiko was still yet unused to saying 'my husband's'.

That's really great.

The change in Reiko's heart was evident in her every word.

Nagare was deeply moved by how much she had improved from being like a sleepwalker since Yukika had come from the past.

Kazu looked at the clock.

'Are you on your way to the airport now?' she asked.

'Yes.'

'I'm sad to see you go, I'll miss you.'

Kazu and Reiko had only known each other for a few months, but Kazu was not just being polite; she was speaking from the heart.

Once upon a time, when she had been extremely averse to being involved in other people's lives, she would not have said those words. Over a period of fifteen years, Kazu had become a parent and there were various aspects of her heart that had changed.

Nagare felt that Kazu's words reflected that change in her heart. *That's really great.* He realized that no matter how difficult life seemed, it could be completely turned around by a single epiphany.

Reiko abruptly stood up from her counter stool. 'Thank you so much for everything,' she said, bowing her head low.

'Oh, not at all,' Kazu replied with a stiff smile, as she felt she personally hadn't done anything.

'If you had something to say to Dr Saki, we'll gladly pass it on,' Nagare offered, feeling a little bad for Reiko that she didn't end up seeing her friend.

After a moment's thought, Reiko replied, '. . . Oh, then perhaps, if it's not too much trouble.'

'Sure, no problem,' Nagare said, standing up tall and straight, to indicate he would responsibly pass on the message. Reiko looked not at Nagare but towards the kitchen behind him. 'I'm also going to be happy,' she announced with clear articulation, and then added, 'Please tell her that.'

'Also?'

For a moment Nagare didn't know who Reiko was referring to with *also*. But that was made clear by her next words: 'I was shown how my happiness was my sister's happiness . . .' Reiko meant that she would be happy together with her deceased sister.

'That makes sense,' Nagare said happily, as his narrow eyes further narrowed.

Kazu was also smiling quietly.

'Well, I'll be off . . .'

After another polite bow of the head Reiko left the cafe, with a look of sweet sorrow.

DA-DING-DONG . . . DA-DING

The bell seemed to ring a lonely chime for a long time.

'You didn't want to say goodbye?' Nagare called out towards the kitchen after a suitable time had passed.

'I'm no good with farewells . . .' said Saki as she appeared from the kitchen. Nagare seemed to have caught on at some point that Saki was hiding because she didn't want to see Reiko.

'But . . .'

'If we ever want to meet, we can do so whenever, right?' she said averting her eyes. She sat down on the counter stool she had used earlier and reached for her unfinished cup of coffee.

It was not that Saki had avoided Reiko because she didn't like her. In fact, she was probably feeling the saddest of them all about Reiko leaving Hakodate. But it was Reiko's decision. Saki wanted to see her off with a smile, but feeling unable to, she had hidden instead.

Taking a slurp of her now-cold coffee, she said, purposely changing the subject, 'By the way, how was Miki?' She was also terrible with the awkward tension that follows after someone has parted.

'Ah . . .' he said as his narrow eyes opened wide.

'You talked to her on the phone?'

Kazu, who had returned from putting the groceries in the fridge, peered at Nagare.

'Uh-huh, ah, yeah.' Beads of perspiration had begun forming on Nagare's forehead.

'Did something happen to Miki?'

'Oh, no. It's not like that . . .' Nagare responded to Kazu's worried response, but his speech was beginning to sound muffled.

'It's just that Miki has a . . .' He faded out and no one caught the last part.

'Eh? What was that?' Saki put her hand to her ear.

'She has a bo-boyfriend . . .'

'A boyfriend?'

'Miki said she has a boyfriend.'

On hearing those words from Nagare, whose right eyebrow was twitching like a character in a manga, Kazu and Saki turned to one another.

A sputtering burst of laughter escaped Saki's lips. 'She ought to be congratulated then, I guess.'

'It's nothing to congratulate her about!'

Saki let forth a full belly laugh at Nagare's impassioned response.

'How old is Miki again?'

'Fo-fourteen.'

'Really? Who is it? A boy from her school?'

'I didn't ask.'

'I wonder who asked out whom?'

'I don't know the details.'

'I wonder if he's good looking?'

'What's that meant to mean? If he's good looking, then it's all fine and good?'

'It's nothing to get angry about!'

'I'm not angry.'

'Hats off to Miki, though, getting herself a boyfriend while her father's not around.'

Saki was clearly enjoying getting Nagare all riled up. Nagare, being Nagare, was growing red in the face.

'I-I think I might go and call again,' he said, and trudged off downstairs.

During the phone call earlier, he had thought it best to play the listening, non-interfering father and hadn't asked any questions. Now, ever since Saki had said 'getting herself a boyfriend while her father's not around', he was feeling very uncomfortable.

'Ah-ha-ha, he's a such dear in some ways, Nagare . . .'

Saki was by no means making fun of him. She was jealous of how among family and close friends such drama is laid bare like that. With Reiko just before, it would have been nice to have not resisted the sadness of saying a final goodbye and openly shed a tear or two. But she knew all too well she could not do that. The endearing qualities of Nagare to which she was referring were the qualities she wanted for herself. She came to that realization as she spoke, and sighed, 'I'm a little jealous.'

'I think I know what you mean,' whispered Kazu.

GO-NG

The clock rang the bell to announce half-past two.

'Hey, wasn't Reiji coming back today?'

After receiving the news that he had passed his audition, Reiji had left for Tokyo the next day to sign a contract with the talent agency and look for a place to live. He had left without a moment's hesitation. There was nothing before his eyes but the dream that was about to come true.

'Yes.'

'Does he know? About Nanako, that is . . .'

'No, I don't think he does.'

Immediately after he left for Tokyo, Nanako had revealed to Kazu and the others that she had been ill for a few years now with a condition called acquired aplastic anaemia. Coincidentally, a donor had been found at this time, and she was to travel to America immediately.

'No, how could he?'

Saki picked up *One Hundred Questions* which Sachi had left on the counter and opened it up to a random page.

What If The World Were Ending Tomorrow? One Hundred Questions

Question Eighty-Seven.

You have a child who has just turned ten years old.

If the world were to end tomorrow, which would you do?

1. Keep quiet about it because they wouldn't properly understand.
2. Tell the truth because you will feel guilty keeping quiet.

Saki remembered this question and thought back to the first time they were posed it. Nanako had chosen 'one' because she didn't want to unnecessarily distress her child.

But then Saki had asked her, *OK, Nanako, if you were ten, would you want to be told?* Nanako had replied that maybe she would want to be told. Her two answers seemed to be clearly contradictory, but even Saki had been satisfied with her reasoning: *I wouldn't mind if I were sad, but I wouldn't want to see my own child sad.* While gazing at that page, she reflected: *It was so like Nanako to care how the other person feels.* On the other hand, the psychiatrist inside her was thinking: *She's the type of person who thinks too much about the other person's feelings and suppresses her own.*

'If you look at it from Nanako's perspective, she didn't want anything to get in the way of Reiji's dreams, but I wonder if Reiji would be satisfied with that.' As Saki was saying this, she didn't think that Reiji would be at all happy about being kept in the dark. It was obvious to Saki, and probably also to Kazu, that the two were in love with each other. But neither of them realized their feelings were mutual.

'Explaining to him about her illness is at least something we can do . . .' Saki said as she closed the book.

'Yes, the other is something for them,' replied Kazu as she gazed out of the window. The *wind flowers* were ever so slowly dancing in the sky.

That night . . .

'Huh?' Reiji blurted out faintly. He was still standing close to the entrance with a bag of gifts in his hands. Nagare, Kazu, Sachi and Saki had waited in the cafe after closing for Reiji's return.

'Acquired aplastic anaemia?' Reiji echoed after hearing the name of the illness from Saki.

'Apparently, after a long search, a donor was finally found for her.'

'A donor?'

The mention of a disease he had never heard of followed by the word 'donor' alarmed Reiji. His mind was blank with confusion. *A long search? How long has she had this illness? Why would she stay quiet about something so important?*

While his mind was still playing catch-up with everything he was being told, Saki continued to patiently explain the disease in a calm manner.

'Acquired aplastic anaemia is a disease where the body loses the ability to make blood from the stem cells in bone marrow, which consequently leads to a decrease in the numbers of all blood-cell types. In other words, it becomes impossible to create new blood, causing difficulties for daily life. Nanako's case was minor, so the effects were not obvious to us. In more serious cases, sufferers can collapse from anaemia and suffer fatigue and malaise, and if left untreated, complications could lead to death.'

'This disease, can it be cured?'

'I'm no expert, so I can't say for sure, but I'd say there's a fifty–fifty chance of a full recovery after a transplant.' Saki claimed not to be an expert, but it definitely seemed like she had read up on the disease.

'Fifty–fifty . . .'

'Yes, well, even if the surgery is a success, the patient's body has to accept the donor tissue, so complications can arise, and the body may reject the transplant. There are fewer cases in Japan, so I think there is a better chance for a successful transplant overseas.'

'So, she's gone to America?'

'That's right.'

Nanako's parents had travelled together with Nanako to America. Since their departure, neither Saki nor Kazu had received any news – there probably hadn't been any spare moments to do so – which left them in the dark as to how she was faring.

'I wish she had told me . . .' Reiji sighed.

'She probably didn't want to worry you.'

'But still . . .'

'She also probably didn't want to get in your way. You had just passed the audition and the future was looking bright . . .'

As Saki said this, Reiji realized, *I certainly have been floating in the clouds.* When he thought back, he couldn't remember what he talked about with Nanako since learning that he passed the audition. He had texted her that he was going to Tokyo to find a room, but even that had been just one-way communication. He had been so caught up thinking about what was happening with him, he didn't even stop to imagine her thoughts as she had written her reply, 'Good luck.'

Considering Nanako's personality, she undoubtedly would be placing her own interests second.

Lost for words, Reiji bit his bottom lip.

His mind kept wandering back to that day when Nanako had worn new lipstick. She had braved the rain that day to take the umbrella to him. He remembered walking with her back to the cafe. Come to think of it, that was the first time he was mindful that they were alone together. He remembered vividly how Nanako's new lipstick shone among the town lights and the flaming crimson leaves.

He also remembered how his heart felt at that time . . .

Without really thinking, he pulled out his phone and looked at the screen. No new messages from Nanako. He found himself getting angry with his phone for remaining silent.

When he focused back on reality, Kazu was standing beside him.

'This is from Nanako,' she said, presenting a one-page letter to him.

Reiji placed his paper bag on the closest table and took the letter. On high-quality Japanese *washi* paper made with real cherry blossom petals, Nanako's instantly recognizable soft handwriting was arranged just like a poem.

Dear Reiji,

Congratulations on passing the audition.

I never told you this before.

No doubt you'll be shocked to hear.

Three years ago, I was diagnosed with acquired aplastic anaemia.

Basically, I can't create my own blood very well.

Apparently, it could impact life in various ways.

If I ignore it – that is.

It also can cause other diseases.

And it could be a whole lot of trouble.

But I found a donor in America,

I'm going there for a little operation.

As we have been friends for a long time, I know I should have told you.

You passed your audition, and I didn't want to get in the way.

I'll never be someone like Setsuko,

Sorry . . .

Not that it's anything to apologize for. lol.

I'm a little scared about the surgery, but I'll do my best.

Please don't worry about me.

You managed to pass the audition on some pretty lousy material.

Must have been a strange whim of the gods.

Go seize that opportunity!

I'll always be cheering you on!

Nanako

The letter was shaking faintly in Reiji's hands.

'I'll never be someone like Setsuko,' he softly muttered just that line after finishing reading.

Well, of course not . . .

Reiji bit his lip as he pondered why Nanako had written that line.

He thought about Setsuko Yoshioka, the childhood friend and wife of Todoroki of the comedy duo PORON DORON, who won the Comedian's Grand Prix. Nanako had been present when Todoroki's comedic partner Hayashida had described what kind of woman Setsuko was and how she supported Todoroki.

Indeed, Reiji shared a lot in common with Todoroki. Originally from Hakodate, he was about to move to Tokyo to become a comedian. He had a connection to this coffee shop and the owner Yukari Tokita, and just as Todoroki was childhood friends with Setsuko, Reiji was childhood friends with Nanako.

So why did Nanako say that she can't be Setsuko? Setsuko loved and believed in Todoroki's talent as a performer and supported him devotedly. Her travelling with him to Tokyo showed how much of a woman of action she was. She knew where she wanted to be in life and was full of confidence. As a fellow woman, Nanako had viewed Setsuko's way of living as cool and appealing.

In comparison, Nanako was indifferent to Reiji's talent. She had watched on as he strove to succeed and supported him no more than any childhood friend would do. She saw nothing that she could do for Reiji, and never thought about going with him to Tokyo.

Yet the difference between Nanako's personality and Setsuko's was fundamental, and they weren't comparable. And unlike Todoroki and Setsuko, who loved each other, Reiji and Nanako thought of each other as just childhood friends.

That's why Nanako writing, 'I'll never be someone like Setsuko,' was so out of character. Nanako had wanted to be Setsuko. If Nanako had never heard the story of Setsuko, she probably would have already told Reiji about her disease, and how she had to travel to America.

But she learned of Setsuko, and she longed to be her. She compared her life to that of Setsuko, who chose to spend her life with the man she loved. As soon as she made that comparison, she realized her feelings for Reiji.

That was why she changed her lipstick that day. She had decided to take a step forward in their relationship. But alas . . . bad timing sometimes causes life to skew off in a different direction. And that was exactly what had happened. Just at the moment Nanako was about to take the courageous step forward to confirm her own feelings, Reiji's phone rang.

It was the email saying that he had passed the audition. If only that email had arrived an hour later, even maybe several minutes later, the two might now be in a different relationship. As soon as he had read it, it drowned out whatever was buzzing in his heart that day.

It was merely bad timing. Without confirming their feelings for each other, one had left for Tokyo while the other, for America. They were too far apart.

Still grasping the letter, his hand dropped slackly. He stumbled dazedly over to the nearest table and sat down.

If only I could contact her . . . I want to hear her voice now. If I could fly there now, I would. But . . .

He didn't know the exact nature of this impulse bubbling up inside him, he found these feelings of being alone and distraught frustrating.

Even if I went, what would I do? Now of all times is not the time to be standing around like that doing nothing. Countless times I failed auditions and each time it felt terrible. But I didn't give up and finally this is surely my chance.

But even now as he was listening to his thoughts telling him to put his own dreams first, when he lifted up his head and saw the letter in his hand, his heart quaked.

But what if I never see her again?

Sometimes you have to make sacrifices to achieve your dreams, right?

Wouldn't I regret it if Nanako died?

But I've signed the contract and already decided where to live. There's no turning back now.

Then why am I so worried?

I want to see Nanako.

What's troubling me?

Which is more important, Nanako or my dream?

I don't know.

What shall I do?

His mind was in a loop, going round and round. He covered his face with his hands and took a long deep breath. Then, at that moment . . .

'Reiji.'

The voice was Sachi's, who was right in front of him. He wondered how long she had been standing there. She was peering into his face with her big round eyes. Sachi must have seen the state he was in and called his name out of concern. And no other reason than that. But it felt to him as if Sachi was asking, *If the world were to end tomorrow, which would you do?*

Sachi had not said anything. But she had read that phrase from the book so many times over the past few months.

'If the world were to end tomorrow . . . ?'

As Reiji muttered this to himself, the old gentleman in the black suit suddenly stood up from his seat.

'Ah . . .'

It was a sight he had seen several times. The old gentleman stood up. He pulled his chin back a little while holding the book he'd been reading against his chest and began walking slowly across the wooden floor to the toilet without a sound.

Reiji's heart raced. He remembered back to a certain day not long after he started working at the cafe.

It was in spring. The cherry blossoms were in full bloom. Still in his third year of high school, Reiji was only working during the busiest hours of the day on Saturdays, Sundays and public holidays.

A man turned up at the cafe and announced his wish to travel to the past so that he could redo his first date, which he had messed up. After Yukari had explained the cafe's rules to him, he promptly left with his shoulders slumped in disappointment.

'Um, is it really true that while back in the past, you can't change the present, no matter how hard you try?' asked Reiji to Yukari after the customer had left. He had been beside them while she had explained the rules. Until that day, he had never heard a proper telling.

'That's right.'

'What use is that chair if you can't change the present? I cannot see the point,' he opined candidly. In fact, he suspected the customer who had just given up on travelling to the past and left had done so upon hearing that rule.

'Hmmm, it might be pointless, I guess.' Yukari didn't argue. 'But some things can change, even if the present reality doesn't.'

'What can change when nothing changes?' Reiji asked in return, just saying the words clearly sounded like a contradiction. 'What do you mean?'

'Well, say you found someone you liked . . .'

'OK.'

'Let's say the girl is beautiful and smart and everyone thinks she's the prettiest girl at school.'

'Oh, OK.'

'But you've never talked with her . . . So do you want to ask her out?'

'What?'

'Do you want to ask her out?'

The question was so out of the blue that Reiji didn't understand. But Reiji actually liked these kinds of questions. He pictured the scenario that Yukari was explaining and answered.

'I don't.'

'Why not?'

'Well, I have never spoken to her, and because such an idol-like girl would never be interested in someone like me in the first place.'

'That's true.'

'What?'

Reiji still couldn't see where she was going. He understood how hypothetical scenarios could be useful. But this was simply too outlandish. Yukari ignored Reiji's confusion and continued.

'Now suppose that one day you heard a rumour that she might like you.'

'What?'

'Well, what are you going to do?'

It was enough to cause a fluttering in his heart, but it wouldn't change anything.

'Um, nothing. It's just a rumour, right?'

'But wouldn't you have a change of heart?'

'Change of heart?'

'Something is surely different, isn't it?'

She seemed to be alluding that it would cause a fluttering in his heart.

'Yeah, maybe a little . . .' Reiji's tone indicated some hesitation.

'Are you getting interested?' Yukari smiled openly, as if she knew exactly how he was feeling.

'Yeah, maybe.'

'Are you starting to think you could go out with her?'

'No way.'

'I see.' Yukari nodded in satisfaction. 'What if you overheard her telling someone you know that she likes you?'

'Huh?'

'What about then? Still not going to ask her out?'

Upon imagining it, his heart stirred even more. The conversation seemed to be playing out as Yukari intended. And frankly, Reiji wasn't that enthralled.

'OK, say that you don't ask her out. Even so, something has clearly changed, right?'

'Yeah, well, maybe . . .'

'The reality that you're not going out with her hasn't changed, right?'

Reiji thought about it logically. Something has changed, but if the 'reality' that Yukari was talking about referred to the relationship between them, it was as she said, unchanged.

'No, the reality hasn't changed.'

'Then, what has changed?'

'Are you talking about feelings?'

A stirring of the heart is a fact.

'Yes.'

'I'm not sure.'

Reiji could understand how the relationship between them does not change but feelings do change. But there was a snag. *Even with this knowledge, is there any point in going back to the past?* He didn't think so. He pouted his lips and let out a protesting moan.

'I understand what you're saying,' Yukari said. 'I don't think anyone returns to the past with that in mind.' She meant that no one goes back to the past to change feelings. 'The important part is what I am about to say,' she continued.

'Even if you find out that it was true that she liked you, the present reality hasn't changed, has it?'

'No.'

'The reality that you and she have not spoken to each other remains the same. You are no closer; you still have no relationship with her. Nothing like that has changed.'

'I guess not.'

'What if she was thinking the same as you? That, considering she had never ever spoken to you, you probably didn't even know she exists. Is there a chance of you two hooking up?'

'Probably not.' Reiji seemed pretty clear about that.

'That would be a shame if you both like each other. So, what would have to happen for you two to get together?'

'One would have to confess to the other, I guess.'

'Right, and what does that require?'

'. . . Action?'

'Exactly.'

Reiji fist-pumped at getting the right answer, and Yukari beamed with satisfaction.

'Nobody gets to be a manga artist just by wanting to be one, right?'

That made sense.

'If it was just a matter of travelling back to the past, anyone could do it. But this cafe chooses people . . . By its rules . . . And some people hear those rules and give up. But those people who are resolved to go back, despite the rules, have a reason for doing so. It doesn't matter what that reason is. If there is someone they must see, or someone they should see . . . even if the present reality won't change . . . then, that's all that matters.'

'Someone they must see even if the present reality won't change?' Reiji tried to imagine someone he would desperately want to see even if reality would not change, but still being in high school, Reiji could not bring anyone to mind.

'You can't picture that person, can you?'

'No, I can't.'

'Well, I guess you will probably have to wait for the time when you desperately want to return to the past even with full knowledge of the rules, huh?'

'I can't imagine that ever happening.'

'I wouldn't be so sure about that.'

Nothing comes about by itself.

The door to the toilet opened on its own without a sound and the old gentleman in the black suit disappeared as if he were being sucked in.

'When . . .'

Reiji stared at the vacant seat left by the gentleman.

'When did she last come to the cafe?'

What could I possibly say to her?

Reiji's mind was oscillating indecisively. But in defiance of his confused feelings, his feet were taking a sure path to the chair.

'I think . . .' Nagare said, looking at Kazu.

'. . . It was a week ago, on the sixth of November, at eleven minutes past six in the evening.' Kazu specified the time with such detail, it was as if she already knew of Reiji's return to the past. 'I remember she was with Sachi.'

'Right, OK, thank you.'

Reiji slowly sat down in *the* chair.

What could I say to her?

But he was acting out of a stirring of unrest that had filled his heart since reading Nanako's letter.

I want to know for sure.

He closed his eyes and took a deep breath.

'Sachi!' Reiji called out to Sachi, who was standing next to Kazu. 'Could you pour me a cup of coffee?'

Sachi's eyes darted up to Kazu and she awaited instructions. Perhaps because it was for Reiji, her eyes seemed to be saying: *Let me do it please!*

'Go and get ready,' replied Kazu. Instantly, Sachi nodded and scampered off to the kitchen, followed by Nagare. He would help with the preparation as per usual.

Reiji had never imagined such a day would come. When the woman had gone back to the past to complain to her deceased parents, and when PORON DORON's Todoroki had travelled back, Reiji had been present in the background, calmly watching things unfold. He had felt like a bystander to someone else's business, a bit like watching the news on TV.

But now was different. He was the one on TV. It was he who sat in the chair. He would be the one who vaporized into nothingness. His heart felt like it was going to explode at any moment. Sitting in this seat, thinking about how

Todoroki must have felt as he was going back to see his late wife, made his chest tighten in agony.

No matter how hard Todoroki tried, he couldn't change the reality that his wife had died. He had lost the one person who had supported him so much. How hard it must have been to fight through this loss to win the Comedian's Grand Prix.

Reiji's mind was once again in turmoil.

What will I do when we meet?

Feeling his heart sinking heavily, he bit his bottom lip and hung his head down. Having finished preparing, Sachi returned from the kitchen carrying the cup and kettle on a tray. Reiji remained perfectly motionless even when Sachi was right by his side.

What will I do when we meet? If I'm going to change my mind, it's now or never. The same doubts cycled back and forth. *And whatever I do, it won't change the present reality . . .*

At this point, negative emotions hung like heavy air around him.

At which point . . .

'Oh, I forgot!' Sachi exclaimed suddenly, and passing the tray to Kazu, she scuttled off downstairs.

Sachi?

As everyone waited in a stunned silence, Sachi immediately returned with *One Hundred Questions* in her hand.

'This.' She held out the book to Reiji. 'Nanako asked me to return it to you.'

'. . . Ah.'

As Reiji took the book, he remembered. Indeed, it had

been Reiji's book originally. He had lent it to Nanako and ever since, Sachi had been using it. Reiji had forgotten such details, but Nanako wanted to make sure what she had borrowed was returned. It was not at all out of character for someone as diligent as Nanako to want to do this, but Reiji thought there was more to it. Into that simple action of returning a borrowed item, he read a message: *I may never see you again.* He couldn't help thinking that had been on Nanako's mind.

'Have you finished the whole book?' Reiji asked Sachi while gazing at it.

'Yeah, Nanako said she might not see me for a while, so we finished it together.'

Just as I thought.

'On the day she came here?'

He was referring to the day he was intending to go back to.

'Yeah.'

'Oh.'

Reiji flicked through the book until his hand stopped at the last question.

'Sachi.'

'What?'

'Can you remember which answer Nanako chose for the last question?'

'The last question?'

'Yeah, the last question.'

I want to make sure how Nanako was feeling.

'Sure, I remember.'

'Which was it?'

'Well, I think she chose "two".'

'She chose "two"?'

'Yes.'

'Oh.'

Just as I thought.

'When I asked her why, she said it was because dying was scary.'

On hearing Nanako's words, Reiji's expression changed.

Nanako had said she couldn't ever be Setsuko. She's probably right. But she doesn't need to be. The person I want to meet isn't Setsuko, anyway. It's Nanako. Besides, Setsuko died but Nanako is still alive.

Reiji raised his head.

We do not know what the future holds for us. I want to see Nanako's face now! What's the harm in that? If she is feeling anxious, what's wrong with wanting to say something to her! I want to tell her it's going to be OK. I want to tell her that she doesn't have to become Setsuko. I don't know the point of saying that, but considering that Nanako goes to America no matter what, then what's the harm in telling her that before she goes? Will it cause strife for someone? No, it wouldn't hurt anyone.

This reasoning flooded Reiji with positivity. He suddenly gave himself two loud slaps across the face.

'??'

Sachi's eyes widened. Reiji's sudden action had startled her.

'Sachi, thanks for telling me that. It's given me courage.'

Reiji had returned to his normal self.

Although he had taken her by surprise, Sachi sensed Reiji's mood had cleared radically compared to his earlier gloomy expression.

'That's OK,' she replied, keen to be helpful.

'Right, I'm ready for my coffee now.'

'Sure.'

Sachi lifted the kettle and whispered:

'Before the coffee gets cold . . .'

A single plume of steam rose from the coffee being poured into the cup. At the same time, Reiji's body became glistening white steam, which rose up and disappeared as if it were being sucked into the ceiling.

It all happened so fast.

Saki, who had been watching silently, spoke.

'Do you think he will confess to her how he feels?' she asked Kazu.

'Huh? Confess?' exclaimed Nagare disbelievingly. 'Why would you say that?'

'Oh really, Nagare, you didn't notice?'

'Notice what? What are you talking about?'

'What part of "confess to her" don't you understand? The two had a thing for one another.'

'What? Really?'

'For goodness' sake, what other reason would Reiji have for going back to the past?'

'It never occurred to me.'

'Nagare, how could you be so blind?' Saki said with an exasperated expression.

'Err . . . sorry.' Nagare's face looked apologetic, even though he had done nothing wrong.

Certainly, Nanako had looked anxious before she had left for surgery, and it wouldn't be unreasonable for Reiji to be speculating on *what ifs*. And in both cases, those feelings might be amplified all the more if love were involved.

'While we were sending him off, I wasn't really thinking about his reasons for going,' said Nagare with a tilt of the head.

'We all could see it.'

'Huh? Really?'

'Couldn't we?' Saki queried.

'Yes,' chimed in Sachi energetically, and Kazu revealed a smile.

'Oh, I see. So that's how it was.' Nagare narrowed his narrow eyes further and stared at the empty chair from which Reiji had departed.

'By the way . . .' said Saki changing the subject. 'What was the final question about? After Reiji heard Nanako's answer, his expression seemed to change.'

In answer to Saki's question, Kazu replied.

' "You are in the womb of your mother, who is in labour. If the world were to end tomorrow, which would you do?" '

'Dr Saki, you never did that question, did you?' added Sachi, looking at Saki.

'No, I didn't,' replied Saki. 'I see, I imagine it is another tricky question. What was option one?' she continued.

'First things first, go ahead and be born,' replied Sachi.

'And the one that Nanako chose?'

'It is all pointless, give up being born.' This time Kazu replied.

'Oh, I see.'

It sounds like Nanako is afraid to die.

'What was on Reiji's mind, I wonder,' Saki whispered as she looked over at the empty chair.

Reiji spent the entire journey travelling back in time thinking about *One Hundred Questions.* He thought of the many questions it asked:

Whether you would return something borrowed.

Whether you would cash in the ten-million-yen lottery ticket you won.

Whether you would go ahead and hold the wedding ceremony.

The more he thought about the questions, he found them to be realistic scenarios that could occur in anyone's life.

What caused a sense of urgency about the questions was the unrealistic premise of 'if the world were to end tomorrow' added to each question.

It made Reiji ponder.

People never know when they are going to die. In fact, Yayoi Seto's parents were killed in a car crash. Setsuko had died from illness. Even Yukika, who he'd worked with, had left this world just a month after being hospitalized.

Nobody can really be certain that they'll see tomorrow.

Reiji was now realizing how important the ordinary life that we take for granted is and how much happiness can be experienced from having someone you care about by your side.

Things that you put off saying until tomorrow are sometimes never said.

After coming back from Tokyo, Reiji realized how important Nanako's presence in his life was – he had been taking her for granted.

Reiji's tomorrow had still not passed.

Nanako was still alive.

It will be too late tomorrow, when the world ends.

But in this world that was not going to end, maybe what he needed to do now was to be honest about his feelings. He needed to forget everyone else and just tell the person who was important to him what was needed to be said.

Perhaps that book is meant to remind us of those things that should be obvious?

Nanako is still alive. He, fortunately, had this cafe in his life. Even if the reality back in the present could not be changed, there was still something he could do now.

There are feelings that should be conveyed regardless of the future. That was why Reiji thought that he would go back to see Nanako even if the world were to end tomorrow.

The sensation in his arms and legs returned, and his surroundings, which had been rushing down around him, gradually slowed to a stop. Reiji touched his restored body to check if it was really there. The billowy sensation had not fully gone, so he just wanted to make sure. Looking around, he saw Kazu at the counter and Sachi reading a book across from her. Nagare was probably in the kitchen. According to the pendulum clock, it was a little past six.

Around the beginning of November, it gets dark early. If

there are no customers, the cafe closes early. The only customers, and probably the last for the day, were an elderly couple seated by the window. He looked around the room but saw no sign of Nanako. There was still a little time before eleven minutes past six, the time that Kazu had specified. Nanako would definitely be there then, as Kazu had said so.

Although Kazu had noticed Reiji's appearance, she simply offered a friendly smile and showed no inclination to strike up a conversation. Reiji knew that this was her way of showing consideration for the person appearing in the chair. He also suspected that she would have realized who he had come to meet the very moment he appeared.

After they locked eyes, Reiji politely nodded and set about waiting for Nanako's arrival. Eight minutes past six – a little longer. He held his hand up to the cup just to be sure. It was fine. Not too hot to touch, but it felt like he had plenty of time until the coffee cooled.

Kazu was chatting with the old couple by the window. They both looked about seventy years old. It seemed to be simple chit-chat, but Reiji had never seen Kazu talking so happily with customers before. Listening in, he heard Kazu call them Mr and Mrs Fusagi. Mrs Fusagi was telling Kazu how she had accompanied her travel-loving husband to Hakodate to see them. They appeared to be regulars of the Tokyo cafe where Kazu had worked. In contrast to the amiable Mrs Fusagi, her husband was silent from start to finish. Reiji couldn't see his expression as he was looking from behind, but he seemed a little socially awkward in his lack of response. Nevertheless,

Reiji was struck by how happy Mrs Fusagi looked as she gazed lovingly at her husband.

Sachi looks like she's reading another difficult book.

Sitting at the counter, Sachi was completely motionless. Reiji knew very well that this was how she was when she started reading a book. So it was likely that she hadn't even noticed his appearance.

It was ten minutes and thirty seconds past six.

Reiji looked at the entrance. *Nanako will arrive soon. Imagine her face when she sees me sitting here.*

Will she shriek in surprise, look at me in stunned silence, or . . .

Oh, she won't cry, will she?

That would be awkward. Now that he thought about it, she might be feeling anxious, it being her last visit to the cafe before leaving for America and all. He might have been flattering himself, but if she had gone to the lengths of writing the letter, he couldn't rule it out. He tried to remember the last time Nanako had cried but found no such memory since kindergarten. All he could remember were times when she was laughing at him or looking at him in dismay. He remembered her ridiculing his comedic material, which he far preferred over some weird insincere praise. So, crying would be awkward – he wouldn't know how to react to that.

DA-DING-DONG

The doorbell interrupted his thoughts. It was eleven minutes past six exactly.

She's here.

As Nanako entered the cafe, Kazu greeted her with 'Hello. Welcome,' and then looked over to Reiji sitting in the chair. As suspected, she had worked out that Reiji was here to see Nanako. She was clearly doing so to make Nanako aware of his presence. Nanako followed Kazu's gaze.

'Huh?'

She had noticed him.

My heart's pounding.

'Er, hi there.'

Reiji gave an awkward salute.

'Reiji, I thought you were in Tokyo? Did you come back early?'

Hey, what!

Reiji felt he was being thrown off script by her overly commonplace reaction.

'Er, no, actually I'm still in Tokyo.'

Because of that, he was now sounding ridiculous.

'Huh, what are you on about?' Nanako knitted her brows suspiciously.

'There's something I wanted to say.'

'Who to?'

'You, of course.'

'Me?'

'Yes, you.'

'Why?'

You're a genius at being slow on the uptake.

'If you have to ask, then I don't know . . .'

Here I was worrying that she might cry. That's embarrassing.

Reiji cradled his head in his hands and sighed heavily. Any other time, it would have been an ordinary conversation.

That is, if he hadn't gone to Tokyo and Nanako hadn't gone to America for surgery.

'What is it with you?'

'Huh?'

'You seem fine with just going off to America while I'm in Tokyo?'

Finally, Nanako realized what was going on. She started frantically jumping up and down.

'Oh god. That chair! What? Don't tell me you've come from the future?'

It was such a typical reaction for Nanako that it was kind of anticlimactic. But Reiji found it relieving.

Much better than looking at an anxious or crying face.

'Oh, if you came from the future, that means you read my letter?'

Little by little, Nanako was grasping what was going on, clapping her hands in front of her eyes at each new point of understanding.

'Why would you go without telling me?' He hadn't come to tell her off, but Nanako's casual attitude was causing him to say critical things.

'Oh, I see . . . Sorry,' Nanako said sombrely.

'No, look, it's fine.' Reiji felt bad for making her apologize.

The old couple Kazu had been chatting with stood up. One would assume they had not noticed the delicate atmosphere between Reiji and Nanako. Kazu proceeded to the cash register, with Sachi in tow, and as they were paying, Nagare came out from the kitchen to see them off. As he did so, he gasped a soft, 'Oh,' as he noticed Reiji sitting in the chair. But that was the extent of his reaction. He obviously had read the situation on seeing Nanako there with Reiji.

After seeing the old couple off, Sachi just waved to Reiji and the entire cafe fell silent. Nanako continued standing a little uneasily until Kazu came over carrying an ice-cream soda and motioned for Nanako to sit down.

'Obviously there is not much time, but make the most of the moment,' she implored, which sounded to Reiji more like a message directed to him: *If you have something to say to her, you'd better do it quickly.*

Looking apologetic, Nanako sat down opposite Reiji. She felt guilty for leaving for – or more accurately, that she was about to leave for – America without telling him.

'I would have preferred it if you had told me.' He meant to sound kinder, but because of his embarrassment, he just sounded like he was complaining.

'I'm sorry.'

'Like I said . . .' *I didn't come here to lay blame on you!* 'I know it's just an excuse, but I've never noticed any symptoms.'

Nanako continued to look down as she spoke in little spurts.

'I somehow thought I'd get cured, and I had wished to be cured. And out of the blue, a message arrived from Yukari saying that she had found me a donor.'

'What? I thought Yukari had been looking for that boy's father?'

'Well, apparently, in addition to that, she had also been searching for a donor for me.'

'I see . . .'

In other words, Yukari had already known about Nanako's illness. Reiji found himself annoyed that he was the only one who didn't know. Nanako picked up on his mood and knew what he was thinking. She quickly added, 'I was going to tell you the other day, but . . .'

Reiji knew immediately that she was referring to the day she had changed her lipstick.

'But you found out that you passed your audition, and it didn't seem the right moment . . .'

'Not really, I guess.' *That's not easy to hear.* 'I behaved poorly, sorry.'

'No, no, it's fine. You just found out that you achieved your biggest dream. My stuff was my own problem, I didn't want to burden you with it.'

She was saying exactly what she wrote in her letter.

If I leave it at this, then what was the point of me coming?

Reiji reached out and felt the cup, frustrated at his inability to be honest with himself. The cup felt less warm than before.

'How's Tokyo?'

'Huh?'

'It will be your first taste of living alone.'

'Ah, yeah.'

'Sorry I can't help out, but I'll always be cheering for you.'

That's her through and through, the same Nanako as usual.

'Stick in there,' she said, reaching for her ice-cream soda.

'Yeah.' Reiji's reply sounded a little disheartened.

Maybe I got myself overly worked up and overthought it.

There was still some time before the coffee completely

cooled, but as Reiji looked at Nanako, it was no longer clear to him why he had travelled to the past.

If Nanako had looked anxious, he could have offered some kind words. But she had just told him to 'stick in there'. Any other time, he could have lightly responded by saying, 'Yeah, you too.' But he couldn't.

Isn't it good she's reacting like that?

It wasn't a bad thing that Nanako was different from how he had imagined . . . that she was behaving as usual. Yet there was a part of him that couldn't honestly be happy about that. To think that he had worried so much, he returned to the past to see her. He felt foolish. But he hated the part of him thinking that way.

I think I might return before Nanako catches on to this weird feeling.

'Well, I . . .' Reiji began as he reached for the cup.

Just at that moment . . .

'This is the last question.'

The voice was Sachi's. But she wasn't talking to them. She was beginning to read a question to Kazu, who was standing behind the counter, and to Nagare, who was busy with closing jobs in the kitchen.

The old couple had left, so Sachi's voice was easily audible to Nanako and Reiji without them trying to listen. Sachi continued.

'You are in the womb of your mother, who is in labour.'

'OK.'

The reply was Kazu's.

' "If the world were to end tomorrow, which would you do?

' "1. Go ahead and be born.

' "2. Don't be born because there is no point."

'Which would you choose, Mum?' asked Sachi with all her childish innocence as she peered at Kazu's face across the counter.

'Hmm, let me think.'

Kazu tilted her head as if deep in thought while proceeding to clean the counter. While Reiji's attention was stolen by the exchange between Sachi and Kazu, Nanako, who was also staring over at the conversation at the counter, said, 'Hey.'

Her voice was still recognizably hers. But unlike up until now, it was now thinner and weaker as though it would fade away.

Reiji looked back at her, but she kept looking away.

'Did something happen to me?' she asked.

What? Reiji didn't immediately comprehend what Nanako meant. He stared oddly at her downcast face.

For a moment the tension was unbearable, then she exclaimed, 'Aha,' with a big grin as if she was fooling around.

'Just joking! Forget I said it, OK?' Nanako grew fidgety, got up from the chair and created some distance from him. 'Won't the coffee get cold? You'd better drink up soon.' She had her back to him, but her voice was trembling faintly.

'Nanako . . .'

In that moment, Reiji understood everything.

Nanako is worried about how the surgery went.

Then he cursed his own shallowness.

It wasn't Nanako who was indifferent; it was me.

Nanako must have been worried about her surgery all the time since he appeared. She must have placed his arrival with

Yayoi, who had gone back to complain to her parents, and Todoroki, who had gone to see his wife, and the moment she saw him, she must have imagined the worst scenario.

In her case, that would mean the surgery failed . . . and she was dead. She must have been thinking that Reiji had come to see her because she had died. She had been deliberately cheerful and carefree to the point of irritating Reiji because of that. She didn't want to know about the future so she was trying to make sure that she wouldn't learn about it. She seemed to want to keep her true feelings from Reiji until he drank the coffee and returned to the future.

But she had let her feelings show. She couldn't keep them concealed.

Reiji had not seen through Nanako's pretence.

'. . . Sorry.'

Reiji had meant to apologize for not reading Nanako's feelings correctly. But Nanako took Reiji's 'sorry' to mean something else.

'Oh god, I don't want to know!'

'You . . .'

We've been together ever since I can remember.

We went to the same preschool, the same kindergarten, elementary school, middle school, high school, and now university.

Being together was normal, I've just taken it for granted.

I've never even questioned why we were together . . .

When did I develop these feelings for her?

When did she develop feelings for me?

Come to think of it, I've never heard about her ever having a boyfriend.

Even though some of my male friends considered Nanako to be attractive, I always thought of her differently.

Becoming a comedian was something I have dreamt of for a long, long time.

I had already decided on going to Tokyo in middle school when I first thought of becoming a comedian.

But hang on a sec?

Was I planning on going to Tokyo alone?

Was I going to live away from Nanako?

We have been together for ever . . .

We went to the same preschool . . .

The same kindergarten . . .

elementary school . . .

middle school . . .

high school . . .

university . . .

and then Tokyo . . .

I've always taken it for granted that we have been together.

I've never once thought it was odd that we were always together.

Hang on . . .

Perhaps I've always liked Nanako. I've just always taken it for granted and simply never questioned it. Maybe my dream and Nanako are inseparable.

I never thought anything of it . . . I never thought to question it . . .

Well I'm going to fix that . . .

'You . . .'

'I don't want to hear.'

'You become my wife.'

'Shut up!'

Yelling with hands on her ears, Nanako's eyes reduced to dots.

'. . . Huh?'

'You, become, my, wife.'

Reiji repeated himself, purposely articulating each word separately.

'That's a lie, right?'

'Why would I lie about that?'

But I am . . .

'What about my disease?'

'What disease?'

'I found a donor.'

'You go to America.'

No one knows the future.

'I go, and?'

'You go, come back, and become my wife.'

After all . . .

'Huh?'

'Congratulations.'

I'm free to say anything. Because my future, our future is ahead of us.

'Why?'

'Why? I want to ask that too.'

And because . . .

'What do you want to ask?'

'Well, you're the one who insisted we get married, you see?'

Whatever I say is not going to change reality in the present.

'I never said anything of the sort!'

'But you do! In the future!'

'Oh, no way would I say that!'

'But you did!'

'You're absolutely lying!'

'Would anyone say something so embarrassing in a lie!'

Would anyone say anything so embarrassing unless they were lying!

'I'm not laughing.'

'I'm used to that!'

'What?'

'But in spite of that, I'm not going to discard my dream. I'll never throw it away. So, I'll go to Tokyo. Life without enough food might continue. But unfortunately for you, you become my wife. I'm saying it happens, so it will happen!'

After saying all this in one burst, Reiji stopped to take a breath. 'That's why . . .' he continued.

'Just stop it!'

I want to do my best and always be with you, is basically what he said. Reiji's inadvertent proposal resounded across the room and at some point, he was being watched by Sachi and Kazu, and even Nagare from the kitchen.

'Phmph,' Nanako chortled unexpectedly.

'Huh?'

What's she laughing at?

'Nice one.'

'It's not a skit.'

'Oh, that's good.'

'What?'

Tears streamed down Nanako's face as she laughed. The tears were gushing out in such big droplets, Reiji looked puzzled. 'Hey . . . hey.'

Nanako looked directly at him.

'Thank you,' she said and stretched out her arms heftily.

Then, 'Oh my! I'm Reiji's wife!' she continued, raising her voice loud enough to take even Reiji by surprise. Her voice was clear, as if cleansed of confusion and anxiety.

Nanako silently looked back at him.

'So, I guess there's nothing I can do to change that future.'

'Yes, that's the rule, I'm afraid.'

'Oh, I see. Gosh.'

'Yeah.'

'Well, there's no changing it, I guess.'

Nanako smiled so wide, it stretched her entire face.

'I choose number one,' said Kazu in reply to Sachi's question. The unexpected timing of her response startled Sachi, who had been paying attention to the exchange between Reiji and Nanako.

That was Kazu's way of signalling: *It will soon be time.*

Reiji, visiting from the future, had to drink up before the coffee got cold.

'Oh, right.'

Nanako also was well aware of the rule.

'Go on. Drink up.'

She motioned to the coffee hurriedly. Reiji was also ready.

He had finished conveying his feelings and there was nothing left that he could think about.

'Yikes, OK, see you.'

With that, he gulped down the coffee in one go. A wavering, dizzy sensation enveloped him.

'Oh, hey, what's your answer to this?'

'Huh?'

Nanako took the book from Sachi and held it out to Reiji.

'What's your answer to the last question, Reiji?'

Reiji remembered. It was the question Nanako chose number two for her answer because 'dying is scary'. Reiji gave his reply while his consciousness was fading.

'I choose "one". I'd go ahead and be born.'

'Number one? Why?'

'I'd be happy to be born, even for only one day, if one day was all I had.'

Reiji's body became shrouded in steam.

'If I get born, then who knows what the future will be? No one really knows. Maybe the world doesn't end at all. That's why I choose number one.'

'Oh, OK,' said Nanako. 'Well, I do too.'

The moment Nanako yelled this out, the steam that had enveloped Reiji's body rose up to reveal the old gentleman in the black suit underneath.

It was unclear whether Nanako's last words reached Reiji or not.

For a while, Nanako simply stared up at the ceiling into which the vaporized Reiji had disappeared.

'Nanako, are you and Reiji going to get married?' Sachi asked inquisitively.

Nanako smiled.

'Well, apparently I end up asking him to marry me . . .' she said, shrugging her shoulders.

Several days later, a postcard from Nanako arrived for Reiji. It was a photo taken after surgery in what appeared to be a hospital room. *I'm fine!* her smile seemed to be saying. Beside her in the photo was an equally smiley Yukari Tokita.

'It doesn't look like Yukari will be coming home for a while,' remarked Saki, looking at the postcard Reiji had passed to her. She seemed to be doubting whether Yukari's story about searching for that man was real or not.

'Yes, it looks that way,' Nagare said with a sigh, sounding half-resigned. But truth be told, Hakodate was beginning to grow on him, and he was beginning to think that it wouldn't be such a bad thing if Yukari didn't return for a while.

'But you have to admire Yukari. She's a truly amazing person, don't you think?' reflected Reiji as Saki was returning the postcard to him. Beside him was a carry-on suitcase and a backpack.

Today, Reiji was leaving for Tokyo. Before departing, he had dropped by the cafe to say goodbye and show them the postcard of Yukari and Nanako.

'She was in that photo twenty years ago, and she helped that woman who was about to throw herself off the pier and thrust her into the future. She was friends with PORON DORON's Todoroki and Hayashida, and she left a note for

Nagare regarding Yukika coming from the past. Now this too, right?'

Yukari was there in the photo together with Nanako.

'I can't help thinking that things might have turned out differently with the Todoroki incident if Yukari hadn't sent the postcards to congratulate the two on winning the Comedian's Grand Prix.'

Reiji seemed to be implying Yukari's actions were like some kind of divine intervention.

'But still, I think they were all just coincidences,' rebutted Nagare, level-headedly.

'I'm not so sure. There's this as well . . .' Reiji held up *One Hundred Questions* and was about to say something when the sound of pounding feet could be heard ascending from downstairs.

It was Sachi. Breathing heavily, she held out a book to Reiji.

'I want to give this to you.'

'Me?'

'Yes.'

It was a novel titled *Lovers*.

'Hey, isn't that your most favourite book? Do you really want to give it away?' asked Nagare.

'Yes.'

Sachi had chosen her most favourite book as a going-away gift for Reiji.

'Are you sure?'

'Uh-huh,' Sachi responded with a smile.

Reiji flicked through several pages of the book. It being her very favourite, she had no doubt taken good care of it.

But nevertheless, the pages were a little dirty around the edges from being read over and over. It clearly was a book that she loved and cherished.

'That was the book that led to your love of books, wasn't it, Sachi?' interjected Kazu.

'Yes,' Sachi replied joyfully.

'But this book is so precious to you . . .' Reiji said, looking at her directly.

Sachi looked directly back at him.

'Well, I read that when you give a gift to someone who is striving to achieve their dreams, you have to give them the most cherished thing you have. Some days, that person who is chasing their dreams will not be able to find the strength to keep going. It will be bitter and painful, and they will have to weigh up their dreams and reality to make a choice. When that happens, the person gifted with the most precious thing will be able to fight on a little more. It apparently helps them to feel they are not alone. So, I'm giving you this book because I want you to fight for your dream.'

'Sachi, how nice of you.'

'Because if you don't fight hard, Nanako's life will be a struggle too,' she added, causing laughter to erupt from everyone.

And with that, Reiji departed for Tokyo.

Several months later, news of Nanako's death reached Nagare, who had returned to Tokyo. It was a spring day when the cherry blossom petals were being blown in the wind like *wind-flower* snowflakes.

After the surgery, Nanako had seemed to be recovering well. However, as was one of the risks of the transplant, her body suddenly rejected the donor marrow. She was taken into surgery again, but she grew increasingly weaker each day. With fever and vomiting and a drug regime that had side effects most people would be unable to endure, Nanako had fought on bravely. Even her parents wondered what was supporting her so strongly, but there is no doubt that it was what Reiji had said that day.

You become my wife.

Several years later, on his fifth attempt, Reiji won the Comedian's Grand Prix.

Standing at Nanako's grave, he held in his hand the novel that Sachi had gifted him and a tatty copy of *One Hundred Questions*. Nanako had been laid to rest high up on Mount Hakodate, close to the graves of foreigners, overlooking the bay.

Before leaving, Reiji left the copy of *One Hundred Questions*. On the last page of the book was an afterword that he must have read countless times. Even the characters had almost faded completely.

On that last page, something had been inserted.

It was a wedding ring.

The afterword on the last page of *What If The World Were Ending Tomorrow? One Hundred Questions* that Reiji had read until it had become old and tattered was as follows.

Something I strongly believe is that we mustn't allow the death of a person to be the cause of unhappiness. The reason for that is simple: if we let everyone who dies be a cause for unhappiness, that would mean people are being born to become unhappy. But the opposite in fact is true. People are always born for the sake of happiness.

Yukari Tokita, Author

BEFORE THE COFFEE GETS COLD SERIES

More than 1 million copies sold worldwide

In a charming Tokyo cafe, customers are offered the unique experience of time-travel. But there are rules and the journey does not come without risks. Customers must return to the present before the coffee gets cold . . .

Translated from Japanese by Geoffrey Trousselot, Toshikazu Kawaguchi's heartwarming and wistful series tells the stories of people who must face up to their past in order to move on with their lives.

What would you do if you could travel back in time?